$\mathcal{A}$ CANDLELIGHT ROMANCE

CANDLELIGHT ROMANCES

PRECIOUS MOMENTS

Suzanne Roberts

A CANDLELIGHT ROMANCE

Published by
DELL PUBLISHING CO., INC.
1 Dag Hammarskjold Plaza
New York, New York 10017

ISBN: 0-440-19621-3

Printed in the United States of America
First printing—May 1978

CHAPTER I

Jamie had walked to the Lodge from the town of Aspen. She walked through the bright winter sunshine, past couples strolling down the winding streets of the picturesque old town, some of them shopping, busily buying equipment for a ski holiday.

And as always, no matter where one went or what one did, it only took a slight turn of the head one way, or perhaps only the lifting of one's eyes from the business of the day toward the horizon, and then, then, there was the mountain, looming, forever there: the great Ajax.

She felt its presence as she walked that morning. The shuttle bus came by finally, and she climbed aboard, along with a dozen or so other people, all rosy-cheeked from the crisp November air, all on holiday.

There was no way at all to determine, here in this most sophisticated of all American ski resorts, if a girl was the daughter of a wealthy banker or if, like Jamie, she was from the Midwest, here working in a bakery or shop. Most of the young people, when not on the slopes, wore jeans and sweaters, and only a fashion expert could tell if they were from an expensive boutique or a chain store. Today, jostling along with the merry bunch in the shuttle bus, heading toward the huge redwood and glass Lodge, Jamie looked as much like a rich, spoiled young playgirl as the rest of them.

Only her eyes said differently. There was a certain look of awe in their hazel depths, a certain wistfulness, that look of the proverbial urchin looking into the candy store window.

The life led by the jet-setters who came here seemed to Jamie to be very much like some sort of lovely fairy tale. She had seen these "Beautiful People," spoken to them sometimes, when some of them were shopping in town and stopped in her aunt's bakery, lured by the delicious aroma of the hot fruit bread baked there. They were usually very good-looking, charming, gay and, it seemed to Jamie, always on the verge of doing something exciting. As she wrapped up the sweet rolls, the hot breads, they would gossip about various people, parties, social events, all of which sounded exciting and fun-filled.

They were, in short, fascinating, as their life seemed to be. Until the previous night, however, Jamie had not even considered staying on here, since her aunt and uncle had put their shop up for sale and departed for Wisconsin. But sitting alone in the abandoned bakery, with its cold ovens and its sad memories, she had somehow decided to stay on in Aspen, instead of going back to her parents' home.

The bus stopped near the Lodge, and along with the others, Jamie got out. At once she felt warmed and cheered by the sight of people sitting around on the wide front porch, wearing ski clothes, drinking coffee or spiced tea or perhaps a toddy. It was refreshing to her; there were no tears among them. She'd had her fill of misery, and now that most of her grief for her younger cousin had subsided into calm acceptance, she longed with all her young heart to be a part of what she now saw spread before her like some kind of banquet—smiling young men, beautifully tanned and teasing, lovely, chic women, flirting, talking, healthy and vibrant. Some of them sat close together at tables, holding hands, even kissing, leaning across cups or glasses to do so. The sun shone steadily on them all, if not warmly, at least with what seemed to be a kind of benevolence.

With this before her, how could she possibly ever go

back to Fond du Lac, Wisconsin, to take some hum-drum job, marry a dairy farmer and settle into the solid kind of life her mother and two older sisters had?

Someone, a young man wearing a white grin and an expensive-looking ski sweater, reached out and caught her arm as she walked across the porch toward the main door of the Lodge.

"Didn't I see you on the south run this morning?"

"No," Jamie said, smiling, "I'm afraid not."

"Didn't I meet you at a house party in Newport last summer?"

"No," she told him. "Excuse me."

Would it make any difference to any of these people if they knew she'd worked in a bakery and came from a farm back East, instead of a finishing school or perhaps an estate someplace in California or New York? Of course it didn't matter; Jamie felt certain that nothing mattered here but the happy pursuit of good times, friendships and marvelous parties and pleasure.

She had been in Aspen since August, three months, and this was her first time at the Lodge. It was proving to be a little like a walk through Wonderland.

"I know you," another young man said, stopping her as she headed for the information desk. "Aren't you—"

"No," Jamie said pleasantly, "I'm not."

She moved on, through the crowd of young people who nearly filled that huge room. At one end of the room there was a long mahogany bar; people sat at it and behind them, others stood. It seemed to be the most popular place in the room, although other people, cou-ples mostly, gathered around the roaring fire in the floor-to-ceiling stone fireplace.

"Help you, miss?" The girl behind the information desk looked up. She, lucky thing, was secure in her job—and, apparently, in her social life. A handsome young man stood nearby; he'd been about to ask her to go out with him. The girl had that look, Jamie noticed, that so many of these jet-setters had—long hair, carefully bleached, cut to perfection so that it looked breezily ruffled.

"I hope so," Jamie told her, "I'm looking for a job."

"You have to be kidding," the blond girl said, her eyes on the broad back of the man as he ambled back toward the bar. "All the seasonal jobs around here have been filled for months. I applied here two years ago and I wouldn't have been hired last month except that the other girl got married to one of the ski instructors."

"I knew that jobs were hard to get," Jamie said, "but I—I had this feeling that I—" Her voice began to falter. She had very definitely felt that a job was waiting for her here in Aspen. She had felt that her decision to stay was right, and if it was, surely the right job would materialize.

"Everybody wants to work here," the girl said flatly, her manner not too friendly. "Sorry, I'm afraid you're out of luck. Unless you want to be the hundredth or so applicant for a job that's probably already taken."

"Those odds don't sound too good." Jamie took a small, determined breath. "But tell me where it is and I'll go apply."

"Suit yourself. It's— Wait a minute." She reached into a drawer and took out a small piece of yellow paper with typing on it. "Here, you take it. But don't get your hopes up because this sounds like a dream job and I'm sure it's filled. I'd have had a go of it myself except that the work only lasts six months."

"Six months!"

The blond girl shrugged. "He's a writer. You've heard of David Saunders, haven't you? They made a movie of his last—"

"Yes, I've heard of him. Thank you very much."

She took the yellow slip of paper, made her way through the crowd and with the scent of expensive perfume, simmering food and damp wool still with her, caught the shuttle outside for town.

David Saunders' leased house in old Aspen was only, as it turned out, a few blocks from the bakery. It was

Victorian, as many of the older houses there were, a big, roomy, gingerbread-with-pomp kind of house, with a circular porch and a heavy, carved front door.

Most of the tourists who rented or leased these houses had a maid or housekeeper, so when the tall man with the beard opened the door, Jamie assumed he was the houseman.

"Hello," she said, "I'd like to see Mr. Saunders, please."

"Sorry, he's busy."

"It's about a job," she said quickly, afraid the door might be shut in her face. "Please—if he hasn't filled it, tell him I'd appreciate it if he'd interview me."

The eyes, cool to the point of being almost icy, regarded her.

"Okay," he said, after a few seconds, "come on in."

The interior of the house was dim, and there was a certain feeling of chill inside, not so much from lack of heat but from the cold fireplace, the faint dust on furniture and the clear feeling Jamie had that this room, the "sitting room," was seldom, if ever, used.

"I prefer interviewing in the kitchen," he said, turning on lamps in the friendless room, "but something's wrong with the heat out there. You can sit over there."

She felt a mild sense of shock. She hadn't thought about the kind of man David Saunders might be, that author of the glittering, sometimes bawdy books that usually dealt with jet-set places and people. Now, confronted by this tall, somewhat untidy-looking man with the brown beard, she suddenly felt a bit awed.

"It's mostly a matter of leaving your name and phone number," he told her, tossing himself into a nearby chair. He wore battered-looking slacks, a T-shirt and sneakers. He was perhaps thirty-eight; the edges of his brown hair showed some silver.

"Yes," Jamie said, "of course." Then, suddenly, she decided to be more open with him. "You don't really seem anxious to hire someone, Mr. Saunders. It might be better if you told me what my chances are."

He seemed surprised by her honesty. He had been busily going through drawers, looking for a pencil, but Jamie's words caused him to turn and give her a quick, interested look.

"I suppose you could say your chances are as good as anybody's," he told her. "The fact is, I haven't yet begun my book. But I'll be starting it any day now. Any day."

"I see. Well," Jamie said, deciding not to get upset if she didn't get this or any other job, "if you hire me, I'm afraid it's going to have to be fairly soon. If I can't find something, I'm not going to be able to stay. But," she said quickly, "I'm not trying to ask for special consideration. A lot of girls need work around here. Everybody isn't rich."

"No," he said, "and thank God for it. Here, put down your name."

She did, and as she handed him the slip of paper, their eyes met and they smiled. It was surprising to Jamie, the way she felt a liking for this man almost instantly.

"To be perfectly frank with you," David told her, "the kindest thing I can do for you is not to hire you."

"*Not* hire me?"

"That way," he said, a trace of a smile on his mouth, "you won't be swallowed up in the daily debauchery of Aspen and its millionaire lowbrows." He got out of his chair restlessly. "Why don't we go to the kitchen? It's cold out there, but I'll light the oven or something. I want some tea."

So she followed him through the house, through the austere dining room complete with ancestral portraits (not his, thank God, he told her), then to a large, chilly kitchen where a solitary coffeepot perched on the old stove. David looked inside, made a face and began looking for tea.

"But I like it here," she said, settling herself at the table.

He turned on the gas jet under a small pan of water.

"What, I'd like to know, is so terrible about one's going back home? I've written books about women who didn't want to go back home, but to be perfectly honest, I've never fully understood why." He sat across from her at the small table. "Maybe you can clear that up for me. You see, I believe I long to go home, only with me, home is forever gone. The people who—made it home are dead. But you can still go back. You've a lifetime to hang around a place like this."

"If you hate it so," she asked softly, "why do you stay?"

He shrugged. "Memories, I guess. And it's a good place to think about my next book."

Jamie nodded. Her decision to try to stay on here had surprised even herself. It was not that she didn't love them all back there, and it wasn't that the greenness of Wisconsin's hills had stopped charming her. It was—something else—

"I think it's because of the people here," she said suddenly. "I think it's the glamour. I know that's a trite word, but it's the only one that comes to mind."

"You're right," he said dryly, "it *is* trite. But then, so are they." He looked at her. "You seem to be a very nice young lady. I usually don't give advice but within the past three weeks, during the time I've been interviewing, I'd say I've said these same words at least ninety-seven times. No, ninety-eight, counting now." He took out a pack of British cigarettes and offered her one. "*Go home.*"

Suddenly, Jamie felt a kind of anger sweep over her. This man was rude, rude, and in some very subtle way, overbearing. Charming, yes, but he had no right to march her out here and order her to leave Aspen!

"Good-bye," she said abruptly, picking up her purse. "Thank you very much anyway."

"Wait—" He stood up, smiling through his beard, his eyes suddenly mischievous. "Who knows—you might be the lucky girl to get to type my next best-seller."

"I don't think so. You're much too anxious to get me

to leave town, Mr. Saunders." She started for the door but she suddenly turned to face him again. "Are you sure you want to hire somebody, or is it only that you like to tell people to go home?"

He suddenly laughed, throwing back his head. When he walked toward her, he put out his hand and caught hers in apology.

"I've been very rude," he said, making a little mock bow. "Please forgive me and stay for lunch. I'm afraid I've nothing very tasty—since the bakery down the street closed, I haven't been able to get—" He stopped suddenly, midway to the refrigerator. "The bakery. That's where it was. I knew I'd seen you someplace, and at first I thought it must have been at one of the local parties, or maybe in the bar at the Lodge. But it wasn't, thank God." He came over and smiled down at her. "It was the bakery."

"My aunt and uncle own it. Or did, rather. They've just sold it. I worked there since August." She suddenly remembered him. He always came in when they were the most crowded, midmorning, when people came off the ski slopes wanting coffee and something warm and sweet to sustain them until lunch.

"Kindly tell them I'm planning to take up a petition to have them come back. I'm not sure I can live without that hot fruit bread they used to make." There didn't seem to be much in the refrigerator, but he finally pulled out four eggs, and with a kind of flourish, began to scramble them.

"They'll never come back here," Jamie said softly. "Their son was killed last winter, on the mountain."

David turned from the stove to look at her. "You mean your cousin was Kurt Carnot, the kid who was killed on Ajax last year?"

Jamie nodded. "His mom and mine are sisters. Kurt was two years younger than I am. We were friends as well as cousins."

"Terrible thing," David said, his manner suddenly kind, not so flippant. "That's a part of Aspen I've grown to hate. And so his parents closed up shop and went home after the accident?"

"They hung on as long as they could. Kurt was killed last March and they left last month. That's eight months. They tried very hard but it was just too much for them, staying on here."

He nodded sympathetically. "You see—I couldn't quite remember when it happened, when that boy was killed. I read about it, of course, but I suppose I felt it was just more proof that life can be cruel to some, kind to others. At any rate, I'm very sorry. What's your name again?"

"Jamie Eden."

He was looking at her with interest in his brown eyes. "You're French, aren't you?"

She smiled. People often asked her that; she was petite, with very dark brown hair and eyes that were sometimes dark, sometimes colored with gold and green.

"My grandmother used to work in a bakery in Paris. That was before she was swept off her feet and whisked off to Wisconsin. I come from a place called Fond du Lac."

He handed her salt for her eggs. A kind of warmth seemed to come from this man; she felt it now, encircling her like some kind of cloak. Inside her, the familiar feeling of tears, deep down and bitter, began to form inside her. It surprised her, this sudden, almost overwhelming feeling she had for her dead young cousin. She realized that her aunt and uncle had not spoken of Kurt after she came there to stay with them. It was if they felt that by shutting off their words, they could shut off the agony of their loss.

So until she had mentioned Kurt just now to this man, her feelings had been very much bottled up inside. Even her own parents had apparently decided to grieve in a very solitary way, not speaking of what had happened.

"Fond du Lac. The End of the Lake. Very pretty."

His brown eyes were warm with interest. "Did your cousin learn to ski there?"

"No, not there. We've a lovely lake but no hills. But there are hills around, some of them five hundred feet or more." The mention of Kurt once again made her eyes turn sad. "Kurt always wanted to ski the highest one. He heard about Ajax when he was very small—he used to talk about it to me."

They were silent for a moment. The feeling that Jamie got from him in that moment was so real, so kind and tender that she realized she wanted to talk about Kurt, about her thus-far pent-up feelings.

"Let me make you some tea," he told her. "Tea is much better than coffee for making people feel better." He was obviously trying to cheer her up. "When I was a child, we used to winter here, in a house they've torn down now. But it was just over there, across the street." He finally found the teapot in a cupboard and began heating water. "My mother was a writer, you know. Poetry, very lovely stuff. She used to let me come in at teatime and sit near her." He smiled at her. "So you see, a lot of people come to Aspen for reasons other than the skiing. Or the wild parties. Have you been to any of those yet?"

"No. Kurt wrote me about them though; he had just begun getting into some sort of social circle. He didn't really like it—I guess he felt it interfered with his skiing. You see," she said softly, "that was his real love. It was always that way with him. He wanted to be the greatest skier in the world."

It wasn't until he'd brought the steaming pot of tea to the table, sliced some stale-looking bread for them, finally found some jam and sat across from her that he asked the question.

"Why are you staying on here, Jamie?"

"Because I—I don't want to go back, I guess." She smiled. "That sounds like a foolish reason, doesn't it?"

"Not necessarily. Depends on *why* you don't want to

go back. Is it because you won't like it there without your cousin?"

She felt her face flush. Was it? Was that a part of it? She suddenly realized he was right; she had grown up with Kurt back home, but here, he'd been dead before she arrived. This place was not laced throughout with memories of their childhood days.

"I guess," she said slowly, "I've been—running. I shut my eyes and see myself working here in Aspen, meeting people, maybe even getting invited to some of the fun things they do." She looked down at her cup. "That sounds vain and silly, doesn't it?"

He reached out and covered her hand with his. "Of course not. You know what I think, Miss Jamie whatever? I think that's a very sound, healthy kind of reaction. I think you're reaching out to grab hold of life once again, after a very bad time. What it probably means is, you're ready to begin living again."

Their eyes met. She felt almost as if she'd been forever released from something that had been holding her back, some shadowy sadness that would not permit her to feel quite at peace with herself. Now, that was gone, just as Kurt was gone. She was alive; she had a right to live and be happy again, only, until she had come to this house, spoken with this stranger, she had not been able to rid herself of the last threads of her grief.

"Drink your tea," he said kindly. "As I said, tea is famous for making people feel better."

The coffeehouse was crowded; young people moved about the room much as they had on the terrace of the Lodge. The place was packed, as usual. Jamie finally found a place to sit, a tiny table far in the back, not big enough to accommodate the groups of well-dressed young people who'd all come in together.

She spotted her friend Donna carrying a tray filled with marshmallow-topped mugs of hot chocolate. She waved, deciding to wait until her friend could come sit down for a moment.

"I get my break in ten minutes," Donna said hurriedly, the mugs still on the tray. "Wait for me. I want to hear about your job-hunting."

Finally, when the two girls sat facing each other, Jamie smiled at her friend. Donna was plumpish, pretty, and she seemed to have an unfailing sense of cheerfulness, even though she'd been working and on her own since she was barely sixteen. When Jamie had been unable to comfort her aunt and uncle, it had been Donna who had, on many occasions, comforted *her*. It was hard to look at Donna's chubby, smiling face without feeling better.

"I think I have good news," Jamie told her. "I might have a job!"

Surprisingly, her friend didn't look delighted. "Better tell me about it, Jamie. I've worked Aspen long enough to know there are a lot of con men out there who talk girls into paying them to get them a job. It's done all the time. I hope you didn't—"

"What I did," Jamie said proudly, "was to have an interview with none other than Mr. David Saunders himself! And he's the dearest, sweetest, kindest person I've ever met, Donna."

Her friend's wise blue eyes looked wary. "Isn't he that writer who puts out that stuff about all the sins of the jet set? He's always putting them down—it's a wonder he has the nerve to live here!" She touched Jamie's hand lightly. "Watch out for him, honey. He sounds like he knows an awful lot about sinning, or whatever you care to call it. I mean, he's got a bird's-eye *view!*"

"I don't know anything about that," Jamie said almost defensively; "all I know is, he made me feel good, just sitting in his kitchen. He'd be wonderful to work for."

For a change, Donna looked almost serious. "I'm not so sure David Saunders is really going to hire someone."

"What?"

Donna shrugged. "I hear a lot of gossip in here, Jamie. A lot of those rich people come in here and, small as it is, it's hard not to hear them. It used to bother me—I didn't want to make Listening to Local Dirt my life's work, but after a while, it made life more interesting." She smiled. "They used to talk about your Mr. Saunders a lot. They were all—awed by him. I hear he got very rich, writing about them." Her face sobered. "And I also heard that now he isn't writing a thing and hasn't been able to for three years, since his wife died."

"But then why—" Why, indeed? Why would he invite all those girls to come for interviews? The ugly thought that he might be—peculiar—filtered into her mind, but she rejected it immediately. He had been good to her, very tender and nice. He was a good man; his eyes couldn't look the way they did if he wasn't. Once the reserve and the faint cynicism had left them, after she'd spoken of Kurt, there had been a clear kindness in those brown eyes.

"Why does he run that ad and talk about hiring a secretary? I've heard them talking about that, too. They say it's better than it was when he was drinking, right after Margo Saunders died."

Jamie felt her heart soften, and for the moment the fact that she very likely had no chance at all to get that job, since in reality there was no job, wasn't important.

"I didn't know about his wife. I mean, I read one of his books, but just the one, and I didn't much care to know about him."

The book had been brilliant and brittle, a searing commentary on a life-style that she had known nothing at all about, and, since she'd been only a senior in high school at the time, wasn't particularly interested in.

"I remember his wife," Donna said, taking quick sips of her black coffee. "She used to come in here. Nice lady, tall, kind of willowy. I have to get back to work now. Remember, don't count on a job from David Saunders. He's supposed to have had writer's block for three years, and some people are saying he's finished as a writer. He really loved that woman."

The memory of her sudden, almost miraculous release from her sorrow over Kurt stayed with Jamie all
the rest of that evening. She fixed herself early dinner,
wrote a letter home without actually saying, but hinting
that she'd probably be back within the week, before she
had to spend her saved air fare.

A good-night call from Donna only served to make
her feel even more certain that, although he obviously
was a wonderful man, David Saunders was in no real
need of a secretary, not when he wasn't producing any
work.

She could not sleep. Outside, the stars were crystal
bright in the black sky, and hanging so low that they
were breathtakingly beautiful. Then, for some reason,
her eyes were drawn toward Ajax, the killer mountain
that had taken Kurt's young life.

Something was going on there, on the mountain.
Lights, there were lights being strung up. Some of them
were not yet put up and some of them hung crookedly,
so that the effect, glistening on the snow, was an uneven
pattern of amber, shooting across the quiet fields.

Jamie watched, legs drawn up under her, sitting in
the window seat of her room over the bakery. The night
was so pure and clear that she could see very well, even
though the figures moved in and out of the trees, working on the lights.

Suddenly, the lights went out and the snow beyond
returned to its color of silver-blue. Then, as Jamie
leaned forward to see, they went on again, all in accord,
all perfectly hung, running far up, up the side of the
great mountain, two rows of them, with a wide berth
between, up the mountain and down.

Her breath suddenly caught in her throat.

A ski run—it's a ski run! Set far away from the
regular skiers' runs, set on the steepest slopes, those
with runoffs and deep holes and pine trees that seemed
to appear suddenly, over a deep dip in the earth, as if
they'd been sent there to kill the unsuspecting skier who
emerged at the top of the dip.

Jamie knew it well. Last August, she had climbed a part of it, and had strewn mountain wild flowers along the path, as well as she could, because long before she'd gotten anywhere near the top of the dangerous run on foot, she'd been forced to give up; it had simply been too wild and steep for her to go farther.

That trail had been the one Kurt had been killed on. And now they were stringing up lights as if it were the preparation for a carnival, as if this were a boardwalk and soon, now, the sweet candy and the popcorn smells would begin to show themselves.

Someone else was going to try to make it safely down that deadly ski trail!

Jamie climbed back into bed, shut her eyes and reached out with her mind for elusive sleep. It came, but not for a long while; it was nearly dawn and the black sky had turned into a lavender color before she finally fell asleep. But the reflection of the amber lights was gone, finally.

The sound of the phone next to her bed woke her up. The sky was morning bright outside her bedroom window; she could hear the daily sounds of traffic on the street below.

"Hello," she said, struggling to sit up in bed. Her yellow bedside clock said nine-thirty. She certainly hadn't gotten much sleep.

"Sorry if you're sleeping in," the deep voice said. "This is David Saunders. I've been trying to reach you for hours."

"I'm sorry," she told him, fully awake now. There was something, some kind of excitement, or urgency in his tone that had gotten through to her. "What is it, Mr. Saunders?"

"It's a miracle," he said at once, "an absolute, sanctioned miracle that I should run into you at this particular time of my life. I can't thank you enough, Jamie."

"Thank me? For what?" She shut off her clock's tiny alarm; she'd planned to get up at eleven and give Aspen one last going-over before accepting the fact that, as

Donna had many times told her, every single job in town was filled.

"We'll talk about that later. In the meantime, when can you report to work? Tomorrow, I hope."

Her mouth nearly dropped open. After everything Donna had told her about this man's mental block, he was surely right when he said a miracle had occurred.

"I can come today if you want," she told him.

"I worked straight through for fifteen hours," he said, his voice throbbing with emotion. "Three years I haven't been able to do anything more than type my name and yesterday, after you left, I sat down and my head began to pour it all out on paper! It's great—it's the best thing I've ever written!"

She was to report for work at his house at seven the following morning. They'd discuss salary then, he told her, but he was willing to pay her whatever she asked.

There was no point, Jamie told herself, in trying to sleep any more *that* day. She'd do well to try to buy some of David Saunders' books and settle down to read them, so she could more or less expect what kind of thing she'd be typing.

There was, she found, a whole section devoted to his work in one of the nearby bookstores. Jamie bought three—all very large and all, she noted, written before his wife's death. Then she made her way past the strolling crowds to the coffeehouse.

Someone was putting up a poster on the light post near the café. Jamie stopped to watch, her heart beginning to beat harder.

It was an ad for the oncoming skiing exhibition, and in bold, bright, scarlet letters, it announced that a young man named Thorne Gundersen would be trying the "death-defying" Silverlode Run down the great Ajax Mountain.

She found herself gazing into the face of that young man. He wore the professional skier's cap, or he had, just before the picture had been snapped. He must have taken it off quickly, because his sun-blonded hair looked damp against his head. The eyes were a clear, candid blue and the wide, sensual mouth was determined. It was a beautifully put together face, like that of a Greek god.

And suddenly she remembered. Kurt had spoken of this man often; Gunderson had been her cousin's greatest hero. Thorne K. Gundersen was not only the son of one of the richest men in the country, he was also an internationally famous ski champion.

You're a fool, Jamie said silently. *You're a fool to try that run, and before long, you're very likely going to be a dead fool!*

CHAPTER II

Within two weeks, Jamie and her new employer had established a daily routine that proved to be suitable to both of them. Jamie came from people who were a part of large families, people who were used to "doing" for one another, so she found nothing at all strange about fixing David's breakfast for him at quarter-past five every morning.

Her second day there, she heard him puttering in the kitchen. The kitchen of the house, that often cold room in the back, was located exactly next to the rooms of the housekeeper and her husband, a loyal but extremely lazy old couple who apparently had worked for David Saunders for a number of years. Their presence in the house had made it possible for Jamie to move into the house and live in, so to speak, with David Saunders.

"You're up early," he said to her that morning; "I thought I was the only one in Aspen who got up before dawn. Want some eggs?"

She looked at the mess he was making of the kitchen. "Would you mind letting me do that?"

He sat at the table, obviously relieved to have the burden of cooking lifted from him. "My kitchen is your kitchen, my friend." He gave her a thoughtful look. "A strange thing has happened."

"Strange thing?" She began looking for an eggbeater. "Oh—you mean your being back at work on your book? That isn't strange; it's natural. Have you an eggbeater, do you know?"

He regarded her with level, darkened eyes. "What I mean is, I'm afraid I'm becoming attached to you."

She looked steadily at the drawer she'd opened. His words had somehow touched a nerve. Almost from the first she had sensed that this was a man she might someday come to love. For the moment, though, what she felt was just a kind of intense *liking* for him.

"Please, let's not do that," she said quietly, busy with the eggs.

"It had to happen, of course," he told her. "You see—you somehow managed, either by miracle or magic, to release me from a bond that was sending me straight to the gates of hell, my dear. That's putting it a bit dramatically, perhaps, but actually my not being able to work simply meant, in everyday terms, that I was slipping deeper and deeper into melancholia over Margo's death. I knew," he said, his voice thoughtful and quiet, "that if I could only get back to work, I could pull out. But I couldn't get my mind tuned into the key, the point, I'd make in my next novel. Do you—understand what I'm saying to you, Jamie?"

Yes, she understood. Here was a man who had, for all practical purposes, been lost. Suddenly he wanted to live. And she had something to do with that. Or rather, her own grief did, her own shedding of that grief. Indeed, it had been a miracle of sorts; she felt it, too.

But that did not mean she was falling in love with David, because she was not.

"I'm thrilled for you," she said, deciding that surely she had been mistaken. How could she for a moment have thought that David Saunders felt anything for her but exactly what she felt for him—friendship and gratitude?

"Okay, then, if you're so thrilled, kindly start calling me David instead of Mr. Saunders, okay?"

And so it had been settled, the fact that he was, as he'd said, dependent upon her in many ways. Breakfast became a time they both began looking forward to, that very early hour when, as David had said, most of Aspen still slept.

Jamie would wake up very early; she'd been an early riser all her life, as many farmers' children are. She would dress in front of the heater, a present from David to be sure her room was warm enough, for the house was old. Most of the time, she wore jeans and a comfortable blouse and sweater, in case her arms got chilly as she typed. By the time she got to the kitchen, though, David was there, sometimes reading over the work he'd done the morning before.

Their day began very early, but it ended more or less in midafternoon. Usually, David began getting phone calls then, some from his agents in New York, some apparently from people living right here in Aspen. Sometimes, if the calls came too early in the day and he was still working, he would instruct Jamie to tell the caller he was busy. "Hang up if you have to," he'd told her grimly; "those vultures aren't going to keep me from my work."

And yet, many of his evenings were apparently spent with those same "vultures."

Jamie's actual work began around ten or eleven, when David had finished for the day. So from the time after she'd finished cooking his breakfast, leaving the dishes, at David's insistence, for the late-rising housekeeper, until the time when she sat down and either typed up his notes or typed up the manuscript itself, there was a span of sometimes as much as four hours.

She chose that time to read his books, the ones that had already been published. To her surprise, there were many more than the latest ones, the ones written shortly before his wife's death. There were others, written when he was single, fresh out of college.

It was in one of those books, the earlier ones, that Jamie found the passage that intrigued her.

She'd been there only two weeks, but even in so short a time, she found herself settled in, comfortable, even happy living here. David was kind and good-natured and his books fascinated her, this latest one as well as the earlier ones.

They'd finished work for the day, and now they sat having tea in his workroom, a combination study and bedroom of sorts, where there were books and papers strewn everywhere and a kind of couch he slept on. The room was always somewhat dim, but today it had been made cheery by a fire the houseman had made.

"I have to talk to you, Jamie," he said suddenly, his tone serious. He was hardly ever serious; that was one of his endearing charms. One sensed, as Jamie did, a deep sense of loss and longing in the man, but even so, he was unfailingly cheerful and charming.

Now, his sudden mood-change surprised her.

"Look," he said, "It's about a character I'd like to bring into my book."

For some reason she felt relieved. It was as if she felt that, at some time or another, David just might imagine himself to be in love with her. He was, she felt certain, going through a very vulnerable time of his life, just finding his way back from a near breakdown. But he only wanted to talk about his work.

"You're the writer," she said, pouring more tea for him. "I'm the typist. By the way, I finished that chapter today, and you also told me to remind you to phone your agent. Sugar?"

He leaned forward in the armchair. "Jamie," he said, "I want to introduce the character of your Cousin Kurt in my book." When she only stared at him, shock coming into her hazel-brown eyes, he went on quickly: "Not as himself, of course. I mean, not using his real name. But I need a tragic figure to—"

She stood up, nearly spilling her tea. "You need a tragic figure! You need a—a character to put in your book and you want to write about Kurt? David," she said, her voice beginning to sound angry, "you can't do that."

"Okay," he said quietly, "sit down, Jamie—please sit

down. Now, just give me a moment to explain, will you? Have your tea like a nice—"

"I'm not a little girl," she reminded him. "And I'm not going to sit by and let you exploit—"

"Now wait a minute!" His voice sounded just as angry as hers. "I'm a writer, not a butcher, remember? I have no intention of exploiting, as you say, your young cousin. I only wanted to—to use him as a kind of tragic figure, the one pure, good element in a place where evil reigns supreme."

She looked into his eyes. He meant what he said; she'd been foolish to jump to that terrible, accusing conclusion.

"I'm sorry, David," she said finally.

"Then it's all right for me to introduce a young boy around Kurt's age who is killed on a dangerous run?" He reached out, taking her hand warmly in his own. "You know I'd never deliberately hurt you, Jamie. You also know I'm very, very fond of you and that having you under my roof is sheer sunshine to me. I heard myself sing in the shower yesterday and it shocked me so I nearly slipped on the soap. I haven't done that since before Margo got sick—it was glorious, feeling happy once again. So please don't think," he said seriously, "that I'd want to reopen a wound for you. I know you're among the happy living again, though; I can sense it. In fact, your own strength somehow helped me—that, and the fact that when you spoke of your cousin, it was almost as if my book were being written for me." He smiled at her. "So only say the word and I'll find another way to resolve my book. Honestly."

They talked about it for a while, sitting together by the fire like comfortable friends, and finally it was decided that, by writing about Kurt, in a sense it was making him and his dream immortal. It was a problem that had been resolved, and once the shock of reading about a young man destined to die on the slopes of an infamous mountain had passed, Jamie once again began to enjoy her job.

She often sat late in his study, retyping his notes or reading one of his earlier books. Tonight, she had curled up in one of the armchairs by the dying fire, a copy of one of his most acclaimed novels in her lap.

"Hello," David said from the doorway. He was dressed to go out. "Still up? Still reading? You ought to be out enjoying yourself."

She flashed him a dimpled smile. "I am enjoying myself. I love this book." She held up the book; its title, *The Way of the Wild Ones*, was printed in bold black leters across the face of the book's jacket.

"One of these times," he told her, "instead of just reading about them, I'll see that you meet them." He leaned against the doorway, regarding her. "I should have done so right away—they'd love you, Jamie."

"Love me?" She shook her head. "There are lots of young girls in Aspen much prettier than—"

"Oh, you're quite pretty enough. Beautiful, actually, when the light catches your face. You've a softness about you, a lovely, sweet, dreamy quality that sets a man's soul to rest." His eyes were tender. "It's a very precious quality, you know. Very few women have it. You do, and my wife did, and yes, my mother, although she had the true poet's tough soul. She was a realist— you, Jamie dear, are not."

"I'm not sure I like what you're saying," she told him. Sometimes, like now, for instance, he made her feel—slightly uncomfortable. It was almost as if she were about to open some magical door and there was David, standing squarely in front of it, barring her way.

"I've marked some of the lovliest passages," she told him, changing the subject. "The one about Aspen in the very early morning—that's very beautiful. It was in this book, chapter—"

"I know where it is, of course," he said. "But you know all about the early mornings around here. One day I expect you'll start beating me down to the kitchen."

He waved at her and left, leaving her to sit pondering that passage in one of the novels. It had been pure and simple, the feelings that came to one on the slopes very early in the morning, before "the earth people" were yet awake. David's hero had told of experiencing feelings that brought him close to God and "nearly at peace with the world, such as he knew it was."

The following morning, a full hour and a half before time to fix David's breakfast, Jamie left the house, dressed warmly in ski clothes, carrying with her the skis she hadn't put on since Kurt's death.

The morning outside, clothed in darkness still, in disguise, as David had said, was very still and cold. Jamie sat on the bench for a moment, adjusting her boots, then she headed for Ajax.

Her plan was to ski only on its safe, lower slopes, those that were close to the Lodge, located at the foot of the mountain. But this early the Lodge was closed and she wasn't too sure of the trails. Nonetheless, she sat outside the Lodge and put on her skis, then stood up and headed toward the nearest trail. She was a good skier, a girl born and reared in snow country, but she was not an expert nor did she ever want to be. But there was a certain feeling she enjoyed having, not the sensation of speed but of beauty, skiing down a slope, the snow and whiteness spread out before her.

She felt that this morning, coming down the gentle slope on the full side of the mountain. When she'd reached the open space near the Lodge, Jamie turned and for the moment surveyed the growing morning in all its enthralling beauty.

David had been quite right—it was lovely. Then, suddenly, like some bright, avenging angel, a figure appeared on the horizon. The sunrise was behind him like some kind of blinding spotlight, coloring the snow, softening it, so that his quick descent seemed more like a ballet than a feat of skill and courage, for he was, she realized, coming down one of the highest, most dangerous runs. It seemed, as she watched, that he sometimes floated in the air, suspended for a few heartbeats like some lovely snowbird. She watched, enchanted.

Then he was down, coming closer, going very fast. He took a wide circle, slowed, then began to coast toward her swiftly.

He was very tall, tall as a Nordic prince; the eyes that looked down at her were of a pure china blue. His face was tanned and handsome; it was a face that was somehow familiar.

Of course—he's the one who wants to ski down the run that killed Kurt!

"You surprised me," he said, still looking down at her. "I didn't expect to find anyone on the slopes this early."

"Neither did I. But it was beautiful," she told him candidly, "watching you come down."

They reached the benches at the side of the Lodge. A light had gone on inside; the cook apparently had arrived. The young man bent to help her take off her skis.

He looked up at her as he did so, his eyes startlingly blue. "Have I seen you on the high slopes?"

"Not me. I'm not that good. Besides, I don't believe in risking one's neck." Then, because she knew he'd find out anyway, since her job with David had given her a certain notoriety, she decided to tell him. "I'm Kurt Carnot's cousin. Perhaps you knew him?"

He looked startled. "Of course—I met him two years ago up in Vermont. Say—I'm terribly sorry about the accident."

"Thank you." She picked up her skis. "Well, have a nice day."

"Hey," he said, "wait a minute!" He had caught up with her. "Don't run away, please?"

"I'm not running. I have to go to work."

His eyes were admiring. She felt a sudden surge of something, some kind of just-born feeling. Sheer animal attraction, but all the same, it was there between them, like a beating, excited heart.

"Have breakfast with me," he said, his eyes still on her face. "Please. I'd like to have a chance to talk to you. It isn't often a beautiful girl waits for me at such an early hour."

If they knew about this, they'd all be here, Jamie thought.

For a time, they were the only ones in the Lodge's dining room. As they settled themselves into a corner, choosing a table by a window, Jamie found herself wondering when Thorne would tell her who he was. Then she realized that he seemed to understand that she would know. Apparently, there were posters all over Aspen bearing his face and the announcement that he would try the treacherous Silverlode Run.

Surprisingly, they did not talk of that run. Instead, Thorne spoke of other places, other runs, other mountains, avoiding Ajax altogether. Finally, over second cups of coffee, as early morning skiers began to filter into the dining room, he looked down at his coffee cup; his voice was candid.

"You're David Saunders' new girl, aren't you?"

Jamie felt her mouth drop open. "I'm—*what?*"

He shrugged his shoulders, wide in the bright ski sweater.

"I understand he's working on a book and that he's got the pretty cousin of Kurt Carnot working for him." His eyes met hers. "Working for him and living in his house."

Quick heat flushed Jamie's face. "I'm afraid," she said quietly, "you're jumping to conclusions."

"Then you aren't his girl?"

"Of course not. I—"

He looked at his watch. "I've a business meeting in fifteen minutes. See you tomorrow, same time, same ski run. Okay?"

Without thinking, Jamie found herself agreeing.

The shuttle bus had begun running and she hopped aboard. There was a feeling inside her—excitement mingled with something close to joy. Was it possible that in so short a time, Thorne could make her feel like this?

She came down like a pinched balloon. It was light by the time she pushed open the front door of David's leased Victorian, and the first thing she saw was himself, sitting gloomily behind his desk in the study, with the door wide open, so he could see her as soon as she walked in.

"I ought to fire you," he said, and at first she thought he meant it. Her eyes flew to the mantel clock—ten-past seven!

She sank into a chair, shaking her head. "I—honestly don't know how this happened. I mean—I meant to get back to fix your breakfast and—"

"Hang the breakfast; it isn't that. It's only that I promised I'd send in that chapter today and I doubt if we can get it to the post office now for the noon delivery out of here."

Jamie took a deep breath. She felt horribly guilty. How could she have forgotten the time this way?

They got back to work, finally, Jamie busily trying to get the typing done by noon, David softly dictating into the machine across the room. Usually, this time was spent by Jamie in reading, but this morning there was extra work to get out, and since she'd begun late, by noon her shoulders ached from the hurried typing.

"I'm a slave driver," David told her, handing her a sandwich. "Here, eat this. I'm afraid I've been terribly hard on you today."

Not at all," she said. The sandwich and noontime tea tasted delicious; usually the housekeeper sent in a lunch tray, but until today, Jamie hadn't enjoyed the food so much. It was almost as if meeting Thorne had revitalized something in her, brightened life up to a point where everything seemed beautiful, everything was fun, food was delicious and the whole day shone with bright promise.

"I must say that whatever you did this morning suits

you," David told her, stacking pages neatly on his desk.
"You've a positive glow about you."

She smiled. "It was all your idea, really. I read how
lovely it is on the slopes in the early morning and I decided to see for myself."

"And?"

"And," she said, her cheeks flushing, "you were
right. Absolutely."

Later that afternoon, David came over to her desk.
He leaned over her, read the page she was working on
and pulled up a chair, close to hers.

"I've decided it's time I turn you loose on the vultures, Jamie." He sipped his first drink of the day.
"They've been very, very curious, you know. For one
thing—most of them never thought I'd be able to work
again. And secondly, to have me back at work, writing
about them and doing it so busily and efficiently that
they probably know it's good, what I'm doing—well,
they naturally want to meet my inspiration."

"I'm not your inspiration," Jamie said softly. "Kurt
is, remember?"

"Nonetheless, they all want to meet you. Why don't
we—"

The shrill ringing of the front door bell stopped their
conversation. David winced, then got slowly and reluctantly out of his chair. Jamie heard the heavy front door
being opened by the housekeeper, then, it seemed to
her, there was a sudden change in the atmosphere, a
different feeling.

The serenity was gone. Definitely.

The young woman was the first to rush into the
study. She was talking as she came, and when she saw
Jamie, she was suddenly silent.

"Hello," Jamie said, beginning to gather up the typed
notes and the carbon of the manuscript. "I was—just
leaving."

"Oh, don't run off now," the young woman said,
coming closer, "we've all been dying to meet you." She

sank into one of the easy chairs by the fireplace. "Any female who could get David to go back to work must have something very—special."

Jamie felt sudden anger begin in her, but she tried hard not to show it. Had there been some implied insult, some hidden meaning in the woman's remark? The eyes that met her quick glance were certainly not friendly; they were cold, the color of silver ice.

David saved the moment; he came in carrying his drink, not trying to hide the fact that he'd been interrupted at his work.

"But this is a special occasion," the man behind him was saying. "The exhibition needs you there, Dave. You're the naughty little boy who writes horrible things about us. We need you."

There was a sudden silence. David had begun to look vastly annoyed; his face had turned a dark uncomfortable color.

"May I present my secretary, Miss Jamie Eden." He put a casual arm around Jamie's slender, sweatered shoulder. "This is my good friend, Miss Rhonda Miles, and this—this is my beloved physician and fellow ice-fisherman, Mel Goodman."

The doctor was balding, about forty, and, except for his bright, intelligent eyes, a clown. The woman in the armchair was red-haired, hard-eyed and beautiful. She was also extremely hostile, or at least so it seemed to Jamie.

"We were just beginning to get a lot of work done," David told them, not bothering about whether or not he was being rude. "I thought I made it very clear at your last boring bash, Rhonda dear, that I do not like to be phoned or visited before the very late afternoon."

The red-haired girl pouted. She had that very special look about her, a look that was almost some kind of stamp or mark. It was, Jamie realized, the look of the Very Rich. It could, perhaps, be imitated and very likely was in many instances, but the look was certainly there on this girl. It consisted of expensive but country-chic clothes, blue jeans and a little-boy-look sweater, and hauntingly breezy perfume and carefully tended, tousled, flaming hair. That was the look of Rhonda Miles. But there was more to her than the look, as Jamie was fast discovering.

She was cunning. In thirty or so seconds, she had made David promise to come to her party, and she'd even managed to get him to smile as he promised.

Only after they'd left, driving off in a bright green Porsche, did David return to his former mood.

"I must be out of my mind," he said. "Now why in blazes did I let that witch talk me into going tonight?"

"Apparently the lady has powers to charm." She slid a fresh piece of paper into the new machine David had surprised her with a few days before. "She didn't seem to have a very hard time convincing you."

"She bewitches people, that one. Honestly, she can put some sort of voodoo on people and before they know it, they're caught."

"Caught?"

"Never mind," he told her. "Anyway, I'll have to call and tell her—" He let his breath out slowly. "Wait a minute! This just might be the perfect moment!"

Jamie just looked at him, unprepared for what he was about to announce.

"This is it," David said excitedly. "This is the night I'm going to let them all have a look at you at last. You're going to meet them all, little girl, the wild ones, the spoiled ones, the evil ones, the miserable ones. I'm going to turn you loose on the Beautiful People!"

CHAPTER III

At first she was not sure that she should go. For one thing, she wasn't at all sure she liked the idea of going to a party with David Saunders, since apparently there was already some nasty gossip going around about her living in with him.

A bit of the awe she had felt for the Beautiful People waned. If they could say things about her like that, when they didn't know her, had never met her until today, perhaps David wasn't being too critical in his books about them.

"You never believe one word I write, do you, Jamie?"

"Of course I do," she told him, busy once again at her typewriter.

"No, seriously. Here I am, practically ordering you to go to that party with me tonight and you don't even act excited." He came over to her, his voice light but somehow worried. "I'd think a girl would have some reaction when invited to attend a party in hell."

"What?" She saw that he seemed to be quite serious.

"When I said you obviously don't believe a word I say in my books, I mean it. If you believed in my great message, Jamie, you won't consider going with me tonight under any circumstances."

He could be very annoying, this complicated man.

"What makes you so sure I want to go?" But she found she could not look at him, into his steady, worried eyes.

"They've bewitched you," he said almost sadly. "And once I hand you over to them——"

"You aren't handing me over to anybody!" She glared at him from her desk, her face flushing. "Frankly, I found that woman very rude and I've no intention of showing up at her house!"

She began typing furiously, glad she'd said that, and pleased that she meant it. It was true; she'd be very, very interested in seeing Thorne once again, surprising him by showing up on the arm of David Saunders. It might even be fun, "accidentally" running into Thorne that way. But the memory of Rhonda Miles' insolent, silver-colored eyes, cold and unfriendly as winter's last days, stayed with her.

No, she would not go to that party, not even though David actually seemed to think it settled that she go wih him.

"One thing is very important," he told her, "and that is for them not to hurt you."

"Mr. Saunders, nobody is going to——"

"David. We agreed on David and Jamie, remember?"

"David, then. Nobody is going to hurt me because I'm not going to put myself in a position where——"

"So you'll have to be dressed to the teeth," he said. "You can probably find something in town that might do, although I doubt it. These women shop in Paris and show it off here. But with your eyes and figure, you'll make whatever it is look great."

She tried to shake her head no; she even stood up and pointed her finger in his face at one point, but it did no good. David wanted her to go and the truth was—she wanted to go.

"You can't possibly buy me a dress," she told him firmly. Her mother would— What would her mother do? Not do, but think, if she knew? "I'll go with you to the party but you'll have to let me go as I really am," she told him.

"Which is poor."

"Yes," she said, smiling a little, "which is poor."

He grinned at her. "I adore you, little Jamie. And I'm going to take you to the Cinderella ball so go and get dressed. It isn't my fault you won't let me wave the magic wand of money and buy you a knockout dress to wear tonight!"

"But what about the chapter? You said you wanted to mail it—"

"The chapter can wait until tomorrow," he told her easily. "This book is going to be so good—in fact, it's already so good that they're going to snatch it right up. You're my good-luck charm, Jamie, and as long as I have you, I'll be rich, popular and successful." He bent down and lightly kissed her cheek, there by her desk. "Go and prepare thyself, lass. Tonight, you take the jet set by storm!"

She sat for a long time in front of the dressing table, there in the upstairs corner bedroom that had been assigned to her. Outside, Aspen had begun its evening's activities; the ski slopes were empty now, with the early darkness, and lights were on in the old houses like this one. Far up the mountainsides, the expensive chalets gleamed with lights; people were having cocktails, dressing, preparing to have a dinner cooked by someone else. One of the richest and most written about families in the world had been spotted on the slopes that day, a politician, his wife and two of his cousins. The town was electrified over the oncoming exhibition and the rush of celebrities who were coming to see it. Even this early, every apartment, every chalet, every house, even every sleeping room—was rented.

All because of Thorne Gundersen, the friendly, blond, sympathetic young man she'd met in the morning moonlight, there on that frozen slope. It had seemed rather like a dream; all day she had not been able to shake that feeling, nor the feeling that the unexpected meeting with the internationally known playboy (for he'd been called that) had caused in her. It had been nothing they had talked about, for their conversation had been mostly limited to his talk of other ski lodges, other mountains, other parts of the country. It had been casual, almost formal conversation, but she'd sensed that he was watching her, that he felt, as she did, some tremendous and unexplainable pulsation going on, as if an inexplicable chemistry had taken place.

The thought of seeing him tonight made her feel almost giddy. She went through her clothes, the ones she'd moved from her room over the bakery to this spacious, old-fashioned room in David Saunders' rented house. There were two dresses she tried on, turning this way and that to look, and seeing only the rather dull color and the provincial cut of both of them. Finally, when it was time to leave with David, she appeared in the study wearing a simple gray tweed skirt and a short red cashmere sweater.

"Jamie," David said, standing up, a martini in his hand, "may I say that you look—"

"I've very sorry," she said quickly; "you see, when I'd tried on both of my—"

"Lovely," he said evenly. "Perfect, in fact. A stroke of genius. The little secretary, the one who brought a dying writer's dead brain back to life, shows up looking like a well-scrubbed schoolgirl. They'll adore you, my sweet. Come on, let's not be too fashionably late. It might be clever, you know, for us to show up on time, instead of having them all standing around, waiting for our grand entrance."

Suddenly she was afraid. The way he put it, the way David talked about it, she'd be walking into a den of lions. Besides, she could imagine what some of that nasty gossip must include: according to all of David's books, people in the world's most sophisticated set frequently, if not often, drifted from sex partner to sex partner, always living under the same roof with their current mate.

Even Thorne had thought that of her, at first. As she remembered, he hadn't seemed at all shocked, either. David was right about one thing, most certainly; they did things a lot differently here from the way they did them back in Fond du Lac!

"Jamie? You look pale—did I say something to frighten you?"

She managed a wan little smile. "You've said everything to frighten me, David. I'm scared to death."

He laughed, putting down his glass and taking her hand.

"Good. You've got a far better chance of surviving if you're scared of them. Don't forget, little one—they're absolutely capable of chewing you up into pieces and then spitting you out. Each and everyone of them is in love with one person only—himself or herself. Their beloved is the reflection in the gilt-edged mirror."

David drove very fast once they were out of Aspen. His car was a smooth little Jag, low and powerfully built. He stepped on the gas as they began to climb the mountain road and the car sped forward like a shot.

The night was clear and very cold, although the car was infinitely warm and cozy. Jamie shut her eyes against the outside beauty and tried to remember just why it was she'd decided to let David convince her to go. A mental picture of Thorne, his china-blue, intelligent eyes watching her over breakfast, came into her mind.

Be honest, she told herself. *You're on your way to that party because you're hoping to run into him.* And somehow, going in on the arm of David Saunders seemed a very good way to make Thorne notice her. Not that he hadn't already, she thought, smiling.

"You're looking very smug," David said from beside her. "I'm beginning to have a very strange premonition. I'm beginning to feel that you're going to be able to survive them all. I think you've got great powers, Jamie."

She opened her eyes, letting the sky and the cold, bright stars fill her vision.

"And I think you've got a lot of blarney."

But she had to admit she did feel a certain strength, a kind of lovely realization that, by a twist of fate, the lonely little girl who was resigned to being forced to go back home was suddenly the awaited-for guest at one of this famous resort's most-talked-about parties.

At least David said it was talked about, and he was the one who knew. On the fast drive up the mountain road, he "clued" her, as he put it, as to whom she'd be meeting.

"Rhonda you already met, and you know her to be a tigress, right?"

"I suppose you could say that, yes."

They were leaving Aspen behind them, winding their way up one of the big mountains, where lighted chalets laced the mountainside with blazing lights. "And you've met my buddy, the doctor. Mel's okay; he's completely sane and very dedicated to his practice. I'd say his only fault is that he likes to hang around with people like Rhonda Miles."

She looked at him quickly. He was basically a kind man, she felt certain. It wasn't like him to talk so unkindly about anyone.

Then, suddenly, she remembered a character from one of his most famous novels. The man had been secretly in love with a woman who was, by any standards, hard and, in this case, cruel. To cover up his guilt for harboring such a love, he continually pretended to loathe the object of a passion he neither understood nor cared to nurture.

It was, Jamie realized with a start, entirely possible that David Saunders felt that way about the rude, cold-eyed, beautiful Rhonda Miles!

It was Rhonda's chalet they went to, a beautiful wood and glass house built on the side of one of the mountains, with Ajax directly north of it. There were cars parked everywhere, in the front and side yard, near the mountain's precarious edge, up and down the road that led to the huge, sprawling house. Rhonda, according to David, owned this house; she made a sizable fortune yearly just from renting it out while she played around in various summer resorts. Her money came, as most of the money in Aspen did, from inheritance; Rhonda's story was sadly like many of the women's thereabouts. Her parents had been divorced for many years and they'd both married many other people in the meantime. Actually, Rhonda had no family.

"Only money," David said grimly, pulling up in front of the chalet. "And look what some of it will buy!"

The front door opened as if on cue and suddenly a woman seemed to half tumble out. Her dress was cut, to Jamie's way of thinking, shockingly low and it was revealingly see-through. A well-dressed man appeared in the open doorway, grabbed her bare shoulders and began kissing her.

"Don't mind them," David said dryly, "they just happened to get drunk a bit early."

As they walked into the foyer, Rhonda seemed to swoop down on them, a drink in her hand. She wore stunningly chic satin pants with a barely see-through, cream-colored blouse that showed off her supple body to perfection. Her flaming hair hung down her back, giving her a certain wanton look as she took David's arm.

"Welcome, darling. I'm sure you'll find a lot of material for your book here tonight. We're all going to be especially wicked for you!" Her silvery eyes glanced Jamie's way. "How nice that you decided to come."

"Thank you." The feeling of excitement Jamie had experienced briefly when the big house had first come into view left her. She definitely felt unwelcome, and her young face must have shown that, because in a matter of seconds, three men came to her rescue.

"All right," David said finally, after eager self-introductions, "take her. I hope I've taught her enough about how to watch out for vultures." He teasingly kissed Jamie's hand. "Enjoy yourself, my dear, and if you need me, you'll probably find me sitting at the bar, drinking only ginger ale, since I need a clear head to work in the morning."

Jamie was brought a drink, which she politely refused, a plate of catered, delicious food, which she picked at, and coffee, which she sipped, her hazel eyes looking around the large room as the three men all tried hard to impress her.

"What did you do for David, getting him back to work?" one asked, his slightly bloodshot eyes admiring. "I'd like for you to do for me whatever it was." He finished his drink. "Was it black magic or what?"

"I'm afraid it had nothing to do with magic," Jamie said, very small in the middle of that masculine circle that had surrounded her. "Mr. Saunders was simply ready to go back to work, that's all. I had nothing at all to do with it."

"I don't believe you," the one in the middle said, leaning toward her. "I think it must have been your beautiful eyes—"

Suddenly her heart seemed to stop. Thorne Gundersen had just come out of one of the rooms, a game room of some sort, followed by a bevy of young women. They were all young and beautiful, and they all wore the unified stamp that said they were rich, spoiled and pampered.

He had seen her too and was now watching her, standing very tall over the eager, bobbing heads of his little groupies, watching her with surprise and then pleasure in those shockingly blue eyes.

They smiled at each other, over the heads of others, the cocktail glasses, the hum of conversation, the darted glances to see who was here and with whom and what was she wearing. Many of the women seemed to be wearing next to nothing, with their expensive, immodest gowns, but Thorne had no eyes for any of them as he made his way toward Jamie, having deftly excused himself to get away from his little admirers. On his way across the room, people stopped him, older women and some men, eager to speak to him, to let others hear them call him by his first name.

Somehow, he broke the circle of men around Jamie and put one strong arm around her waist almost intimately.

"You always seem to turn up at just the right time," he told her, then, bending to her ear, he whispered, "Let's get out of here."

CHAPTER IV

"I can't," she heard her own voice saying, "I—couldn't possibly."

He had put his arm around her waist and he was skillfully but steadily moving her out of the men circle, into the crowded, busy room and across it, toward the wide, glass patio doors. When they reached these, he turned her rather swiftly around so that she faced him, holding her lightly in his strong arms, his tanned face just inches away from her own.

"Of course, you can. You can do absolutely anything you choose to."

A woman in a see-through dress that exposed her breasts completely came up behind Thorne, sliding one pretty arm around his wide shoulders. He turned to her, annoyed.

"We were just leaving," he said, grabbing Jamie's hand.

But halfway across the room, toward what looked to be a hallway, David swooped down on them. His face, Jamie saw, looked very annoyed, as if somehow she had done something wrong.

"There you are, Jamie dear. I've some people waiting to meet you. They're panting to meet the magical girl who got me working again." He nodded pleasantly enough to Thorne, but his eyes seemed to hold a cold warning. "How are you, Thorne? I haven't seen you since that evening in Paris. Magot's, wasn't it? You were with a model or something."

"I think she could be classified as Or Something,"

Thorne said, smiling. "You don't mind if I borrow your secretary for a while do you?"

"I mind very much indeed," David said lightly. He took Jamie's other hand. "There are at least twenty people gathered over there waiting to meet her. So if you'll kindly excuse us—"

The feeling rising inside Jamie suddenly identified itself: it was anger.

"If you don't mind," she said, holding up both of her imprisoned hands, "I'd rather not be carted off by either of you!" She managed to smile politely at them both. "Excuse me; I'm going to the ladies' room."

She felt a definite sense of indignation, walking away from them. She had been nervous about coming here, nervous once she got here, and now she was beginning to wish fervently she had not come at all. She had often thought of parties, when she lay in bed in the little room over the bakery. Her aunt and uncle always retired early; even so, there would often be the sounds of her aunt's sobbing on into the long night. Gradually, after the pain of her cousin's death began to wane somewhat, Jamie would find herself thinking of the happy parties being held in those lovely mountainside houses, wishing that, instead of lying in the narrow little bed, listening to the sounds of weeping, she could be happy again, full of life again, able to laugh again. The parties had seemed so exciting to her back then.

But now that she was actually present at one, it was somehow all wrong. The women were, some of them, coarse and loud, their not-always-pretty bodies shamefully exposed to the men. Most of the people there seemed rather drunk and silly to her.

Halfway across the room, a tall, friendly young man with large glasses grabbed her arm and asked her if she wouldn't like some grog.

"Some what?" She glanced behind her, over to the far side of the room. David was walking away, away from Thorne; his back looked stiff and rather angry. And Thorne headed straight for the bar, side-skirting

Jamie, not looking her way. At the bar, he threw his arms around the shoulders of two girls, both of whom looked up at him adoringly.

"Grog," the young man said. "It's really a whammo of a drink."

"No, thank you," she said, and somehow she got away from him, across the wide, beautiful room crowded with milling, drinking, laughing, calling-to-each-other people, out of there and through a door and into a sort of hallway where it was dim and quiet.

She leaned against the wall and shut her eyes. Somewhere deep behind them, there were tears of outrage. Outrage? *What on earth,* she asked herself, standing there in that welcome, quiet sanctuary, *is the matter with you? You have two wonderful, interesting, fascinating men pulling at you and here you are, looking for the ladies' room so you can get away from both of them!*

She looked around her. The sleeping part of the huge, sprawling house was evidently here, in this wing. Some of the bedroom doors were open, and as if by invitation, Jamie walked down the quiet, polished marble hallway toward the bedrooms. There, in the first one with an open door, she leaned in the doorway and surveyed the room. It was huge, with a wall of glass on one side, so that there was a magnificent view of the mountains and the town of Aspen. But there was a certain coldness about the room, not in the air temperature but in the expensive-looking furniture. It was like a showroom; one got the feeling that nobody had ever slept in this room.

They treat me like a child, she thought suddenly, and she realized that was it; that was why she had left them both standing there, and that was why she had suddenly felt miserable and didn't know why. Both David and Thorne had behaved as if she had no mind or will of her own, as if she had to make some kind of idiotic, childish choice between the two of them, as if the idea of whether or not she would go with Thorne or remain with David meant something so important that she could not possibly be expected to decide it for herself.

She walked into the silent room and sat in front of the small, mirrored vanity. Her gold-green eyes met themselves in the mirror.

Be very careful, she told herself silently. *You must be very, very careful or else you're going to get hurt*. Thorne could do that to her; she sensed it. She had felt some kind of pain, not physical but hurting, when he'd gone over to those two pretty girls and put his arms around them.

She let her breath out, tugged at her fluffy, short hair and stared at her reflection. Her face was pretty enough "for all normal purposes" as her mother used to say sagely. But she was no gloriously beautiful woman; there were many others at this very party who looked a lot lovelier than she did, and who were probably very rich as well.

Why then, was the handsomest, possibly the richest and most certainly the hero of the hour so interested in her?

She found David waiting for her at the end of the hallway.

"Kindly don't scold me," he told her. "You upset me, you know, running off like that."

"I only went to the ladies' room," she told him. He held open for her the carved wooden door at the end of the hallway; she passed through, and then she was back in the huge room where the party was.

"Nonsense," David told her, taking her lightly by the arm, "you were furious. Come on—they're all waiting for you." He turned to look at her. "Jamie? Something wrong?"

She swallowed. "Yes," she said slowly. "I can't—I'm afraid I don't want to meet them. I mean I don't want you taking me over there by the arm or hand or whatever—guiding me, pushing me over there so they can all look me over. As if," she said, her voice wobbling a little, "I'm some kind—of lucky charm, and you want to wave me in front of them. David," she said steadily,

"I did not cause you to write again. You would have anyway. So kindly stop thinking of me as some kind of—magic!"

He took his hand from her. "Then you don't care to meet my friends?" The voice was controlled, low-pitched, but the brown eyes were frosty.

"I didn't know," she said quietly, "that they were that—your friends. Not long ago you called them wild, spoiled, evil—and I think you said miserable." She touched his wrist. "David, all I'm saying is that I'd like you to let me meet your friends by just—*meeting* them, the way everybody else seems to be meeting people at this party. I'm sorry," she told him, "but I just don't like having people talk about me as if I've cured you of something!"

His eyes shut. He was silent for perhaps two heart-beats, then he looked at her with renewing warmth in his brown eyes.

"Bless you, Jamie. You have the most amazing effect on me, do you know that?" He touched her cheek gently with one finger. "No, I don't suppose you do know it. But it's as if you can calm me, set my thinking straight again. My wife used to do that and so did my mother. I never—thought I'd find it in a woman again."

"Then don't be angry," she said softly, and she turned and left him there. She walked straight toward the corner of the room where Thorne was. He was watching her approach him, the blue eyes taking on a look of surprise then pleasure. Jamie was stopped three times on her way across that noisy, smoky room; each time it was by a young man who wanted to flirt with her.

Thorne came forward, leaving the women who had been gathered around him, chattering.

"Ready to leave now?"

She smiled up at him. "I'm sure something good can come of this party. I'd like trying some of the food, please."

They moved toward the lavish buffet; his hand was on her arm.

"I want to talk to you someplace. Alone, away from here."

She turned around to face him, a plate in her hand. His blue eyes were serious, not teasing, the way they'd been earlier.

"I'm not at all sure I want to leave," she told him, turning back to the row of silver dishes; chafing dishes kept warm by glowing fat candles; chilled, cut-glass bowls of salads with what seemed like endless dishes of sauces; vegetables cut in the shapes of flowers, leaves, animals; dishes and cups and saucers of foods that Jamie didn't recognize, filled with wines and spices and herbs. "It's rather like a Roman feast."

"Instead of dancing girls, we have—"

"Groupies," she said promptly, carefully spooning a dark brown, curry-laced sauce over wild rice. "Your faithful admirers."

She heard him chuckle. "I'm not sure about you," he told her, beginning to fill a plate for himself, moving along with her from one gleaming, aromatic dish to the next; "I didn't think you'd be so independent."

"Well, I am," she said, and then she protested, laughing, as he loaded glops of bright colored wiggling gelatin onto her plate. "Not that," she told him. "I know what that is. I only want to taste the things I haven't tasted before."

They found a relatively quiet corner in the game room, which contained bookshelves lined with brightly jacketed novels and a pool table, and, as in the other room, a bar with a white-coated young man serving behind it.

Thorne put his plate of food down on a low table in front of them; he seemed more interested in watching Jamie eat hers than in any of the food on his plate.

"Have you ever driven down the mountainside this time of night?"

"Of course. I have friends here in Aspen; I'm not

exactly a stranger here." She didn't tell him that the only time she'd ridden in a car here at all had been with Donna, who drove an ancient wreck back and forth to work at the coffeehouse.

"I was hoping you'd say no. I wanted to be the first to give you that pleasure." His eyes met hers. "Please, let's leave this place."

"And waste all this delicious food?" But heat had risen to her face; an excitement was generating inside her. This man had some kind of power over her; whenever he came near she began to feel quite differently from, say, the way she felt when David walked into a room where she was.

"All right," he said, "eat your salad or whatever it is. But I promise you, I don't give up easily." He settled back, watching her enjoy her food, his blue eyes looking at her as if he were enchanted.

The doors to the room opened, and as they did loud music and talk came into the room. A fattish woman wearing very tight, bright green pants and a lot of jewelry swept in, spilling her drink on the young man with her. He looked at her angrily, then smiled and dabbed at his jacket with a napkin. Jamie suddenly remembered two of the characters in David's current novel—an aging, willful woman and her paid-for lover, who secretly despised her.

"What is it?" Thorne asked suddenly.

"What?" She turned to look at him. "Nothing. I mean—I guess I thought I saw someone I knew."

So they sat there, eating their food, drinking aromatic coffee and, although not rudely, watching the people who walked, whisked or stumbled into the room. Everybody seemed very merry and friendly, as if they were all part of a large, strange family.

"You're disappointed in them, aren't you?" He put down his cup.

Jamie didn't answer him. A man who had been playing pool with a blond girl suddenly slapped her across the face. There was a hush in the room, then, very quietly and steadily, the girl began to curse him.

"Seen enough of the jet set for one evening? Come on," he said, "let me take you down that mountain road I told you about."

Jamie felt as if she were suspended, as if her Self had slid out of her body and she stood watching, seeing herself—a slender girl with short dark hair and a rather wistful face, sitting with a plate of food on her lap, looking into the incredibly blue eyes of that big-shouldered young man.

"Yes," she said finally, "I'm ready to go now."

His car was parked far down the road; he told her at the door that he couldn't find her coat; there was no time; if they were to get away without being noticed, it would have to be quickly.

He had put his own sweater on her, a very large, warm thing, and now, hurrying down the road under his arm, she suddenly stopped and looked up at him. She felt almost giddy, almost as if she'd had some kind of wild wine that had made her feet light and her heart joyous.

"Thorne—what on earth are we running from? I mean—we've a perfect right to leave the party if we want to! So why—"

Lights went off in two of the upstairs bedrooms. "Because if we don't," he said darkly, his voice mocking, "they'll catch us and we might never be able to find this night again. So let's go."

They ran. His little sports car, the silver color of the snow around them, seemed ready to tip over the mountainside; but Thorne, after telling Jamie to wait by the road, got in it, started it and, back tires spinning, urged it onto the road and then to Jamie.

He reached over and held the car door open for her. "I think we're going to make it." The car shot forward, made a dizzingly quick U turn and shot down the mountain.

Jamie didn't speak. The first feelings of fear that had risen up in her as they rounded the mountain curves got lost in a new sense of danger and excitement. At any given second, they could easily go off that dangerous, slippery road, and yet she felt absolutely certain they would not. She sensed that this man handled cars as well as he handled himself when he swept down mountainsides like some kind of beautiful, avenging angel.

But halfway down he suddenly began to feather the brakes instead of swooping around the curves hell-bent. Jamie, sitting silently beside him, felt a vast sense of relief as the small car assumed a more normal speed.

"I'm sorry," he told her when the lights of Aspen were just ahead of them, "I shouldn't do that—drive that fast. It isn't fair to whoever happens to be riding with me."

"It's all right," she told him. "In fact, I have to confess I enjoyed it." She turned to look at him. He seemed to be hunched forward in his seat; his eyes were squinting against the reflection of the brightly lit, moonswept snow. "Is something wrong?"

"What's wrong," he told her easily, "is that it isn't fair for me to do my test-driving thing when I have a passenger." He glanced fully at her as the car stopped at a cross section leading directly into town. "Especially such a lovely one."

There was something in his mock-serious tone that reminded her of David's way of talking to her. Was there something wrong with her, that men didn't seem to want to take her seriously, but instead treated her as if she were a very charming but gullible child?

They were driving through the town of Aspen; lights were mostly off in the downtown, and instead of its daytime look of activity, there was a certain loneliness about it at this hour. Except for the sandwich shops that stayed open late, there would be few places that did any business at all. People entertained in their own lavish homes, leased or bought outright; some young people who worked at the Lodge sometimes sat over weary cups of coffee in town cafés, but not many.

It was a town where, as David had said to her, if you took the very rich away, there would be nothing left. The pulse beat of the places was geared to them, their wants, their buying power. There was a place called the Silver Queen, farther down, Topsy's, then Satisfaction and the Quick Bite. The darkened shops showed goods made by Indians: turquoise and silver, tooled leather and rugs and blankets, little drums for children and lovely sepia prints. Antique shops with tiny lights in their windows displayed everything from Victorian lamps and old photographs to aging skis once used by the local Indians.

But all of it spelled money, just as David had said over and over in his books.

Thorne's little car came to a sedate stop at one of the town's red lights. He turned to look down at her; his eyes held a look she didn't understand. Moments before, they had been rushing down a mountainside— there had been a certain closeness between them, brought from the party, still there as they sat side by side, speeding away from the others, down the mountain toward someplace where they would be alone.

But now, the closeness seemed to be gone. Jamie realized this, looking into those blue eyes that seemed to have chilled.

"I think," he said carefully, "we've made a rather bad mistake."

It was foolish, she told herself, to let his words have such a strange effect on her. It wasn't only humiliation at his sudden change of heart, it was thinking about how rude of her it had been even to consider leaving the party in the first place.

She stared at her hands there in her lap. "Yes," she said, "David was kind enough to take me and here I am—some kind of would-be runaway." She let her breath out. "I don't know what made me decide to leave that way. My boss especially wanted me to go and I—"

The light had changed, but the car didn't thrust forward. Thorne stared out the windshield, his profile outlined in the soft light from outside.

"I don't really want to take you back there," he said.

"But you just said—"

"Will you come and have coffee with me at my house, Jamie?" He had turned to her; his eyes were no longer cold but almost pleading. "Okay, so I shouldn't have taken you away from the party and okay, so I drive too fast for the wrong reason and yes, I know you had no right to leave that place because David just might get so angry at both of us that he'll fire you." He leaned closer to her. "But if he does, please come straight to me."

His lips lightly brushed hers, sending a thrilling feeling of excitement surging through her like a shot. When they were again driving on through town, she realized she was trembling. This man excited her more than any other ever had, and yet, there was something, some silent, intangible thing, wrong, and she knew it. One minute, she could almost believe he was falling in love with her, and the next minute, he would suddenly seemed disinterested.

Take his asking her to come with him tonight, for instance.

"The house has a very nice view," he told her, and now he was being very, very charming, smiling into her eyes, a dimple suddenly creasing his cheek. "And I have some very beautiful music," he said, bending forward, closer to her mouth once again. "I'd love to dance with you, Jamie."

"Coffee sounds great," she said, her breath coming a bit fast. "But I'm not at all sure you won't change your mind again, before we get to your house."

"Look," he said earnestly, "my mind didn't change." He turned left, leaving the town's main street behind them, heading once again toward the mountain range on the far side, toward Ajax. "I was trying to think of you, honestly. It isn't often I do that—think totally about what's best for someone else besides myself." His hand, warm and without a glove, reached for hers there on the seat. She felt another burst of some unnamed emotion that was very pleasurable rush through her as his flesh touched hers and his fingers encircled her own protectively. "You do that to me," he told her quietly, the car gaining speed, but not that wild, reckless kind of speed he'd showed her before. "It's a totally new experience," he said. He passed a truck, gauging the distance, suddenly silent as his car shot around in front, then slowed again. His hand refound hers. "I'm not sure," he told her, "if you're very good or very bad for me."

Thorne's house sat at very nearly the top of one of the lesser mountains, directly facing Ajax. To sit in his living room on the low, beige-colored sofa was to face that great mountain directly. It was as if one could not avoid the face of it in that place; it was simply there, looming, beyond the glass walls of the front of the house. To escape, to get away, it was necessary to turn a chair around, lie the wrong way on a bed or simply turn one's back to the great mountain.

Jamie had done this as she stood at the portable bar preparing to pour brandy for both of them. Thorne crouched by the enormous stone fireplace, getting a glow at first, then finally a roaring, blazing fire going. The whole room took on a golden look, soft and seductive.

"Try the peach," he told her. "It comes from Château Lemoine in the Bordeaux region. It's very good."

She picked up the bottle and looked at it. It bore Thorne's family name, written in red, on one side of the label. He suddenly looked a little embarrassed.

"My father's place. He died last year, so I suppose it's mine now." He took the glass she held out to him. "I haven't been there, but I suppose it's very beautiful."

"You haven't been there!" She sat down beside him on the rug. "Do you mean to tell me you own a vineyard with a house and everything on it and you haven't even looked at it?"

"You're a very strange girl," he said quietly. "You have an uncanny way of making me feel as if I'm missing something very important. I simply haven't been to Lemoine because——" he shrugged. "I suppose because I don't know what I'd do with myself there. I couldn't ski, so I don't know what I'd do with myself."

"Well, I know what I'd do," she told him, getting quite comfortable, sitting close to him. "I'd walk. I'd walk through the vineyards and I'd reach out and—— touch the grapes. I've always wanted to do that." She put down her glass. "My grandmother used to talk about the vineyards. She was from Paris."

There was a small silence between them, but it wasn't uncomfortable. She felt relaxed, warm, delightful. Moments later, when the sound of throbbing, somehow lonely music filled the room, she really wasn't surprised. So far, the night had been unreal, dreamlike, such a change from her usual life-style that she almost felt as if she were someone else, some different, vibrant, exciting girl who had been given a kind of power she'd never had before.

Thorne's arm had gone around her. Then, slowly, he bent his body closer to hers, drawing her close to him. Her heart was pounding against his chest. As he kissed her, a wave of desire swept over her with such intensity that she trembled. She was lying on the rug; Thorne's mouth sought hers again——

"The phone," she said suddenly. "Thorne, the phone is ringing."

"Damn the phone," he said in a husky voice. "Jamie——"

She struggled to sit up. "Please answer it." She turned her face away from his. There were a thousand tumbled emotions churning around inside her.

"I'll get rid of them," he told her, getting up. She

heard his voice, there across the room; there was a long pause, and when she sat all the way up and looked at Thorne, she saw that he was holding the phone far away from his ear.

There was the faint sound of someone yelling on the other end of the wire.

Finally, Thorne hung up the phone. His face was flushed, whether from the passion of a moment before or from new anger, she couldn't tell.

"That," he said evenly, "was your boss. Mr. David Saunders wants it known that if I don't deliver you safe and sound to his house within the next ten minutes, he's going to come up here and blow the top of my head off!"

CHAPTER V

It was, of course, ridiculous for David to try to force her to leave this way, but Jamie was somehow glad for his wild, irate phone call. It gave her a chance to think straight, or try to; around Thorne, that was almost impossible.

She went over to the phone and gently took it from the furious Thorne.

"David? I'm perfectly well and I'll be along very soon, I promise. You needn't play Dutch uncle because there's—absolutely nothing wrong going on here." She didn't look at Thorne.

"Are you saying I should drive on back to my house and leave you in the clutches of that womanizer?" David's tone was half-teasing, half-serious. It wasn't difficult, however, for Jamie to sense that he was both angry and worried about her having left the party with someone else.

"I'm saying I'm just fine and I hope I haven't offended you by leaving your friend's house."

"Rhonda is no friend of mine, dear. We despise each other. The point is, I don't think it's quite time for you to be adopted by one of the men in Rhonda's little world. I suppose," he said thoughtfully, "I should have known it would happen, once I let them get a look at you. Maybe we ought to have a nice, quiet talk, the three of us."

"David—I'm fine, honestly!" She was beginning to feel a bit embarrassed, with Thorne standing there looking angry and annoyed, right by her elbow.

"You're sure?"

"I'm sure, David. Good night."

"Well," he said reluctantly, "good night, then."

The mood, she saw at once, was totally ruined. Thorne went over to the bar and poured himself a drink.

"Shall I take you home at once, Jamie, or would you care for one of these?" He held out his glass, then drained it. It bothered her, seeing him drink; she remembered how her cousin had always said it was a lethal combination—a ski run and alcohol.

"I'm in no particular hurry," she said, as pleasantly as she could. "It's very lovely here."

Their eyes met; they smiled and he came quickly over to her.

"Come on," he told her, all the anger gone from his handsome face, "sit by the fire." They settled themselves on pillows strewn about on the floor; Jamie lay on her stomach, facing the fire, her small face propped on her hands.

"Why do you do it, Thorne?"

He was close beside her, there on the floor. "Do what? Ski?"

"Ski the way you do. I never totally understood my cousin's passion for it—it was something he never tried to explain to me. But I imagine it's something that one doesn't like to—talk about." She looked at his quiet face, there close beside hers. In the softness of the firelight, he suddenly looked very much like a small, lonely boy. Jamie ached to put her arms around him, to feel his head against her breast.

The urge frightened and disturbed her. She got to her feet and went over to the window, where Ajax stared silently back at her, cold, deadly.

"The place where young men die," she said quietly. Then she turned to face Thorne. "Have you thought about the fact that you may only have days to live? That you might not make it down Silverlode Run, that you might die there like my cousin did?" Her voice was soft, her emotions at that moment were not clearly defined. Later, later she would think about this night with Thorne, think about what it meant in terms of her own life.

"Of course I've thought about that." He shrugged. "It's something I want to do, that's all." He held out his hand. "Come back and sit by me, Jamie. I want to talk about you."

"I think," she said carefully, "I'd better leave. It isn't because of David's call—it's—"

"Of course it's because of David's call. You're afraid of me now, and you weren't before."

"I'm not afraid," she said, her chin rising.

"Then you'll come again?"

"Of course."

He let her out in front of David's house; they did not kiss but the feeling of wanting to was so real that, upon finding her house key and being let in by Thorne, Jamie actually felt weak, spent, drained, as she slowly climbed the stairs to her bedroom.

"Well," a voice said from the darkness below, "you took your sweet time." He switched on the lights and she turned to face David, who stood, wearing his smoking jacket, in the downstairs hallway. "Are you all right, Jamie? You look—"

"I'm fine," she said, pushing back her hair. "Just tired."

He frowned. "Something is changing, isn't it?"

He had put it very well. Yes, something was changing—she had never before experienced such overpowering emotions as she had felt when she was close to Thorne.

"Good night," she said. "I'll see you in the morning, David."

His eyes looked very kind. "Sleep late if you like. Perhaps we'll find a moment to talk. If you don't mind Dutch uncles, that is."

* * *

She slept a dreamless sleep, waking up to winter sunlight spread about the room and the delicious aroma of frying bacon and perking coffee. Jamie stretched, arms over her head; suddenly she felt absolutely marvelous. Thorne was just as excited by her as she was by him, just as interested in being with her as she was with him. She shut her eyes. *Now what? Where do we go from here?*

There was a soft tap at the door and before Jamie could say a word, David's housekeeper came in carrying a tray. There was a winter rose in a slender silver vase, bacon and toast under a china dome, and thick blackberry jam, imported from France, in a cut-glass jar.

In short, it was a very elegant breakfast, but with a sudden sense of shock, Jamie glanced at her bedside clock and leaped out of bed.

"It's quarter-past ten!" She'd be fired—David would be furious!

"Relax," the housekeeper said kindly, "Mr. Saunders told me to tell you to take the complete morning off. He said he had plenty to do and you could catch up on the typing by working this evening." She poured coffee from the silver pot. "Work," she said, "is better than anything else. He said you'd understand his meanin'."

"I think," Jamie said grimly, "I'd better get on down to his study." She gulped the coffee hastily. "It was a lovely tray, and I'm sorry I can't stay to enjoy it, honestly." She was heading for the shower.

Maybe David had given her time off, but she felt certain he was annoyed, perhaps even angry with her, about the night before.

It would be best to get things settled between them at once.

She found him behind his desk, typing away furiously. Knowing better than to disturb his working moments, Jamie went across the room, opened the window a bit and let the shades up enough to allow some natural light to come into the somewhat messy room.

"Why aren't you up there sleeping your head off?"

He glared at her from over his amber-colored glasses. "Didn't you know I gave you the morning off?"

She smiled. She somehow felt relaxed around this man; her head and heart stayed quite calm, unlike the way they reacted when she was with Thorne Gundersen.

"I thought we'd best get it over with," she told him, sitting behind her desk. "Are you angry with me?"

He let his breath out. "No. But I am worried. However," he told her, "this is neither the time nor the place to discuss things."

"David, there's nothing to discuss!"

He poured coffee from the electric pot, taking her a cup. His brown eyes were candid, there behind the reading glasses.

"Are you telling me to mind my own bloody business, by any remote chance, Jamie?"

She felt her face flush. She looked up at him, then down at her steaming cup of coffee. "Yes," she said finally, "I suppose in a way—I am."

"Very well, then," he said crisply, "I'll say nothing more about any of this." He was back at this typewriter when he looked at her again. "When you want a detailed rundown on what makes your new boyfriend behave as he does, let me know."

"I wouldn't," Jamie said a bit icily, "dream of listening to any gossip about Thorne."

"Suit yourself."

The typewriter began clacking away. Jamie, now beginning to wish she'd taken advantage of David's offer to remain upstairs in bed until noon, began retyping some of yesterday's script, but even though this was only the second read-through of the chapter and she loved the book—she found her mind wandering.

She had asked Thorne last night why. Why he wanted to conquer Ajax—what made him feel as he did. And he had dismissed her question, saying he wanted instead to talk about her.

She mentally shook her head, trying to get all thoughts of Thorne to leave. Then, concentrating on the work before her, she allowed her mind to be charmed and interested in David's book.

Time went so quickly that the sudden appearance of the housekeeper with a food tray surprised her.

"It looks very nice," David said, "but I'd like to take you out to lunch today, Jamie." He was putting the cover on his typewriter. "I know a charming place half-way up a mountain. The cooking is very French and very gourmet. Want to?"

She glanced at the phone. "I—I turned down the most lovely breakfast tray this morning," she said. "It wouldn't be right, turning down the lunch tray, too. Why don't we eat here?"

"One might almost think the lady awaits the ringing of the phone," he said dryly. "Very well, then. But let's have some wine to go with things."

Jamie drank buttermilk, but David's voice got warmer and his tone more inspired as he sipped the dry white wine and ate his fish.

"I've been thinking in terms of another book," he said, "something about living. Life; that would be my message."

"Sounds interesting." She sat across the small, some-what wobbly table from him. Outside, it had begun to snow; flakes pressed against the long windows of the house, white and soft. What, she wondered, was Thorne doing at this very moment? Was he perhaps still asleep in that house up there on the mountain? Or was he out on the run, practicing for the big event?

A sudden chill went over her. David was looking at her with dark, serious eyes.

"Are you in love with living, Jamie?"

"Of course." She moved in her chair. "Of course I am."

He was watching her. "Was your grandmother's name spelled Jamais by any chance?"

"Why—yes."

"And you were named for her?"

She leaned forward. "How did you know?"

David smiled. "I just had a hunch, that's all. You like to talk about her, you know, about her life in Paris, things like that. Was she a great beauty?"

"Grandmother was—yes, I suppose you could say she was very beautiful. But," Jamie said softly, "she was much more than just that."

David's eyes were watching her. "Tell me about her. Tell me her flaw."

Jamie looked up. "Flaw? I don't think she had any." She saw the intentness in his eyes. "David, do you mind if I tell you I'm very well aware of what you're doing?" She smiled fondly at him. "I've copied enough of your manuscript to recognize how clever you are at getting people to trap themselves into saying words they don't mean to say."

"Which is another way of saying I have an uncanny way of getting people to tell the truth."

Her face flushed. Suddenly she felt sure this conversation had something to do with her behavior the night before.

"I finished that chapter," she told him. "I'll work as late as you want me to, in order to make up for—"

"Was your grandmother a romantic, Jamie? Would you say she was that? Did she leave Paris because a man wanted her to by any chance?"

"Yes," Jamie said, suddenly annoyed, "all right—she was probably very romantic. But Frenchwomen are, you know."

He smiled. "On the contrary, most of those ladies are very businesslike about marriage. So your darling grandmother was different, just as you, little one, are different." His voice was quiet. "You are one of those unfortunates who is capable of a very deep and lasting love affair. And because you are that—you're very likely to get hurt very badly. I'd like to prevent that, if I can."

"David," she said uncomfortably, "please—will you stop worrying about me?" She took a small breath. "I promise you—I won't neglect my work again, the way I did by oversleeping this morning. I'm very sorry about that and it won't happen again."

He passed her a plate of buttered scones. "Then you don't want an astute, intelligent writer's insight into the young man you seem to be so taken with?"

"No," Jamie said, "I don't."

Which of course was not true in the least. Jamie very badly wanted to know about Thorne's drive, his reasons for risking his life so easily, so offhandedly. But she wanted to learn those reasons from Thorne himself.

It was twilight when she finished her work for the day. This was always a special time of day; work was put aside and very often Jamie and David sat together having a quiet drink, chatting about his work or about various things. The light in the room would be amber and shadows would appear and leap, brought into view because of the burning logs in the fireplace. Jamie loved to sit comfortably in this room and watch lights go on up on the mountainside.

She suddenly realized that from the window to her right she would be able to see lights go on at Thorne's place, up the mountain.

"You're very pensive," David said from behind her. "Thoughtful, I might say. I've been sitting here most of the day trying to get some words together in my head."

There was a sudden shower of light in that house where Thorne lived. Standing at the window, Jamie felt a sudden chill go through her. *He hasn't called today. I thought—I really thought he would.* She felt suddenly lonely.

"I said I'm trying to get some very important words together in my head." David's voice came from behind her.

"Oh—sorry." She turned around to face him. "You mean you're thinking of tomorrow's chapter just now?" She accepted the drink he handed her, something sweet and only vaguely tasting of alcohol. "I thought you said you never worry about tomorrow's work today."

"I'm not," David said, "talking about my book. I'm talking about asking you to go with me on a sort of trip."

Her eyes widened. "Trip? You mean—vacation?"

"Now wait," he said hastily, "I know it doesn't sound exactly decent, but it is, I assure you." He put down his drink. "I'd like to finish my book in Jamaica."

"Jamaica!"

He seemed very serious about it. "I've a place there; I often go there when I'm really deeply involved with a book. Naturally," he said, his back to her now as he began putting crackers and cheese onto a plate, "I'd want you with me. I've become very dependent on you, as I'm sure you know by now." He sounded matter-of-fact, even businesslike.

"David—I—I honestly don't know." She felt uneasy, vaguely frightened, as if some monumental choice had been handed to her. "If you're really deadly serious about leaving Aspen and going to Jamaica, I'll have to think about it."

He came over and, as a father or brother might, gently opened her mouth and popped a bit of cheese in. "Will you consider it?"

"Yes, of course."

But later in her room, soaking in a hot tub, she began to relax. Her feelings about Thorne bothered her; it was not like her to feel such emotions so quickly. Jamie had been in love before, twice, in fact, although she didn't really count the first time because she had been seventeen and had very badly wanted to fall in love with someone.

The second time had been a period in her life when she simply had not felt at all like herself. She had suddenly become radiant, cried a lot, mooned about the house, as her mother put it, and lost weight when the boy unexpectedly joined the Navy and was sent at once to the Great Lakes naval training center near Chicago.

Perhaps David had been right when he called her a romantic.

She looked at the phone, sitting out there in the bedroom, placid, silent. And up on the mountain, the lights from Thorne's chalet blazed like beacons; he might even be having a party. Whatever had very nearly happened between them the night before evidently meant nothing at all to him.

Of course she would go to Jamaica. Why on earth not? There was, after all, nothing to keep her here in Aspen—

Someone came heavily up the stairs. Then, a tap on Jamie's door and the always-cross-sounding voice of David's fat housekeeper:

"You've a phone call; he's dialed Mr. Saunders' number instead of the unlisted one he had put in for you."

"Thank you," Jamie said, and she tried very hard not to skip down the stairs to the black, waiting telephone in David's study.

"Yes?"

"Hello," Thorne said smoothly, as if he hadn't kept her waiting all day for a call. "I hope you're in the mood for dinner."

"Thank you, no." Was she turning him down? Jamie realized that, once again, all sorts of mixed feelings were churning around in her. "I just had a snack with David," she told him. "I'm not at all hungry."

"Well, then, how about a drink? Two, maybe."

"People who ski ought not to—"

"Kindly don't lecture me."

"Sorry." Why was it going badly when she had been waiting to hear from him again?

"Do you want to see me again, Jamie?"

She was silent for a heartbeat. "Yes, I do."

"I'll pick you up in twenty minutes. Oh, incidentally, tell your boss the reason I called his number was to talk to him. I'm going to punch his face when I see him. Tell him that, will you please?"

He hung up before she could say anything.

Something, something was wrong. Yes, she was totally attracted to Thorne; she had never before experienced such an attraction to a man. And he felt that way, too—at least he seemed to.

Then what was it that made her feel uneasy talking to him? She frowned. When would she begin to feel easy with him, the way it ought to be with people—the way it was with David and her?

She was dressing when she heard David's car pull away, out of the old brick garage in back that had once been a carriage house. At least, she thought with relief, David wouldn't be around when Thorne came to pick her up. It was hard to believe Thorne was really looking for a fight, but it was entirely possible.

David was a gentleman; he wouldn't refuse to fight, and would very likely get his nice-looking face smashed in by Thorne.

She put on warm, nicely fitting black wool slacks and a pretty, hand-knit ski sweater her mother had sent her from Wisconsin as a gift. Her cheeks glowed a warm, soft color and her eyes looked more gold than brown or green in the soft light of her room. Outside, it continued to snow.

Thorne was twenty minutes later than she thought he would be, than he said he would be, but if he noticed, he didn't apologize.

"I know a great place where we can sit and hold hands and lose our hearing," he told her. "We might even be able to dance if you like having people stand so close it's like cattle in the pen."

He was talking about Friday's, a disco place nestled at the end of one of the downtown side streets. The activity took place mostly in the basement of the huge old Victorian house; upstairs, expensive, intimate suppers were prepared and served. It was said that an internationally famous skier from Germany had given a party there, the night before he skied to his bloody death trying to make it down the Silverlode Run of the great Ajax.

That had been forty years before.

It was a private club; Jamie realized that when a tall, good-looking young man wearing a casually expensive suit glanced suspiciously at Thorne, then, seeing who it was, grinned and stuck out his hand.

"Haven't seen you for a while, Mr. Gundersen."

"I've been on the slopes, man, on the slopes. Now, I'm giving myself a brief rest due to a case of sun blindness." He put his arm around Jamie. "This is my best girl."

"Very nice."

Jamie smiled, feeling vastly uncomfortable. From beyond them, in a darkish room that smelled of perfume and cigarette smoke, came the wild beat of disco dance music. People moved about, dancing very close; some of them were in each other's arms, eyes closed, seemingly oblivious to anyone but each other.

Inside the room, Thorne bent close to her, his eyes dark blue in the dim light.

"Stay with me. If anybody asks you to dance, tell them your boyfriend will sail them right down the mountain if they put a hand on you."

He found a table for them, far in the back; Jamie suspected it had been saved for him. They were by a window; outside the snow lay clean and serenely quiet, a contrast to the wild music and the restless dancers.

"Terrible, isn't it?" He put his hand over hers; it was warm and very strong. "Terrible place to bring one's girl."

She tried to smile at that, but suddenly she saw that his eyes were serious and her heart seemed to stop for an instant.

"I'm not anybody's girl," she said lightly.

"Yes, you are," he said, and he put his hand on her face. Jamie closed her eyes; even the loud music didn't change the rising feeling in her when he touched her this way.

"Well," a girl's voice said, "if it isn't Thorne G. with a brand-new item!"

"Lydia, aren't you out of your neighborhood? I

thought you only hung around writers on the Left Bank. Jamie, this is Lydia Markin; she's a gossip writer. Makes her living by telling nasty, untrue stories about people."

The girl with the long, sleek black hair, beautifully streaked with bleached silver, gave Thorne an amused look.

"I got bored with Paris, dear, and I came over here to spy on idiot men who get some kind of sick thrill out of going down a very steep hill on two little slat boards." She glanced at Jamie. "I've heard something about you. I've heard you're a witch."

Jamie tried to sound friendly, even though she was beginning to like this place less and less.

"I'm only a witch on weekends," she said lightly. "During the week I work as a typist."

"More than a typist, I've heard." The woman's voice was somehow nasty. "I hear you did something to David and suddenly he's working again. You must have some vastly marvelous secret." She smiled. "One as old as the world itself."

"Now wait a minute, Lydia." Thorne's voice was angry. "I've never hit a woman," he said quietly. "Not yet."

The dark-haired woman stood up, still smiling. "Hitting women isn't in this season, lover. Well," she told Jamie, "lovely meeting you, dear."

Jamie watched her move into the smoke and darkness of the room.

"I take it you don't much like her."

"I've no taste for women who should have been born sharks. Would you like a drink, Jamie? Everything is terrible here."

"Then why did we come?"

He took her hand again. "Do you know—that's a very good question. Let's leave. Let's go to my place. Will you?"

Her heart began beating very hard. "I don't— Maybe we'd better stay in a crowd."

His blue eyes deepened. "I won't touch you; I won't come anywhere near you unless you ask me to, okay?"

"No, it isn't okay. I just think we'd better not—"

"I'll even cook for you. Did I tell you my mother used to be a gourmet cook and she taught me how to cook fish over an open fire? The fireplace at my place does a very nice job on mackerel with saffron seasoning."

His face looked very boyish and honest; his hair had slipped onto his forehead a bit. Without thinking, Jamie reached out and pushed it gently back.

"How could I turn down a meal like that?"

She did not know clearly just what she expected to find at Thorne's place high on the mountain, leftovers from a cocktail party, perhaps. But she certainly didn't expect to find a shower of glass all over the floor by what had been a glass door leading to an outside porch, with a breathtaking view of the sweeping valley beneath.

"Watch out for glass," Thorne said, turning on the lights. "I had a little accident before."

She took off her coat, settling herself once again on the long couch facing the mountain, just as she'd done the night before. Twenty-four hours had gone by and, she realized with a mild start, most of them had been spent with Thorne around the edges of her mind. Even when she'd been doing her work for David, she had found that from time to time her mind jumped back to this room, with its casual elegance, the long, gleaming window and the huge fireplace.

Someone had put up plastic over the place in the window that had been broken.

"Did you cut yourself, Thorne? It could have been very serious."

He was making a fire, quickly, with great precision. "Only a scratch on my arm. Stupid of me to think the door was open. I was going out onto the porch for coffee and I walked right into the glass. There, it's going now."

He had settled himself next to her on the soft, low couch. It was almost impossible to sit up straight on that sofa; it was made so that leaning back was the more natural position.

"I'm glad you came back here with me," he said, his voice warm. "I'm glad you didn't let David talk you into not coming. Did he try?"

Why was David Saunders being brought into their intimate conversation, as if somehow he belonged there as a part of her romance with Thorne?

"I work for David," she said quietly, "that's all. I'm sure I'd be at his house, probably reading tonight, if you hadn't called me." She frowned. "I don't like what some of those people are saying about David and me. It isn't fair. He's a wonderful man and simply because he's come back to life in a way—doesn't mean that I had anything to do with it."

He had a fat, round glass of amber brandy in his hand. His blue eyes looked at her over the rim.

"You're magic, you know. I knew it from the start. You can weave spells around people."

"That's not very funny," she told him.

He settled himself against some woven pillows. "Even your name is magic. If I remember my schoolboy French, it means 'never.' Or maybe it's 'ever.' I hope," he said softly, "it isn't never. For us to never—that would be terrible—" He was kissing her. She realized this with a kind of surprise, then a feeling of sweeping delight. It was a very expert kind of kiss, getting deeper, gaining in feeling, the kind that could easily end by shaking the earth under her.

"I can tell you exactly what it means," she said, pushing him away, turning her face from him. It means 'Never, not ever, at no time whatever.' They used to tease me about that."

"Are you angry with me because I kissed you?"

"Of course not."

"Good." He gently put his hand at the back of her head and slowly, deeply, kissed her again. "Never—at no time whatever—you surely don't mean that, do you?"

Her eyes were closed. "You promised you wouldn't—"

He was still very close to her, his mouth so close to her own, but his eyes had shifted so that he was looking toward Ajax.

"I know," he said quietly, "maybe eat, drink and make love isn't the answer after all."

She sat up straighter, still in his arms.

"The answer to what?"

"The race," he said. "The big, long, hard race. Look—would you like a drink? I think I'll fix myself one."

Jamie realized suddenly that once again, in a split second's time, they had become strangers. The moment of closeness was gone.

CHAPTER VI

They'd had coffee and some kind of sweet rolls which he said a friend of his had sent up that morning, and then, while it was still quite early, he drove her back to David's.

"There's some kind of thing going on at Cassie Belsham's," he said, just before Jamie got out of his car. "Will you go with me?"

His invitation took her by surprise. She had thought that, for whatever reason she didn't understand, he had decided not to see her again.

"Would you mind telling me why you want me to go to whatever-her-name-is's party? I thought you'd decided the brief, merry life wasn't for you."

"I want to see you again. Will you go? Frankly, I've been trying to think of someplace to ask you to go to, and I suppose Cassie's party is as good an excuse as any." He leaned closer to her, his elbow and arm around the back of the seat. "What I decided was not to try to talk you into doing something you might not be happy about later on. But that doesn't mean I don't want you near me, because I do."

Pleasure filled her. Perhaps she was beginning to understand some of his strange moods; at any rate, now she felt she could weather his being polite but remote one moment and then charming and loving a short time later.

"I won't be free until I finish typing up David's daily work. Then I could go."

He smiled into her eyes. "Good. Give me a call when you're ready."

He kissed her good night at the door, and as Jamie let herself in with the key David had given her earlier, she suddenly saw movement of some kind in the dark living room to her right, off the main foyer.

She found the light switch and flicked it.

"David!"

He was wearing pajamas but no robe, and his feet, rather long, skinny ones, were bare.

"I'd just come down for a glass of milk," he told her, "when I saw the car. One can't be too careful about break-ins around here."

He had started toward the stairs and was halfway up when she spoke to him from the hallway.

"You were spying on me and you know it." She sounded scolding.

"My dear, dear child—" He didn't turn around to face her.

"David," she said, beginning to come up the stairs, "you know perfectly well it's true! Look—would you mind telling me why you dislike Thorne so much?"

Finally, he had turned to face her. His brown eyes had a rather thundering look to them, as if he were about to make a long and loud speech to her, reproving her like the Dutch uncle he seemed to want to be to her.

"Yes, I'll tell you," he said. "I dislike him very much indeed, because I happen to like you very much indeed. It's as simple as that. There's something wrong with him; he's got a kink of some kind in him, some kind of—murderous, self-destructive drive, and in the end it will hurt you, Jamie, wound you." He touched her cheek. "I don't want you to be hurt."

Suddenly, he seemed very dear to her, like some tall, kindly cousin, or maybe a brother. Jamie leaned against him, putting her head against his chest.

"I know it seems very quick and maybe even very foolish to you." She took a small breath and felt his protective arms go around her. "I've never felt like this before," she said softly. "I'm not really sure how to be-have—"

At that moment, the door at the end of the stairs flung itself open. The housekeeper stood there in her long nightgown; her embarrassed husband stood in the background.

"I'll be leaving you in the morning, Mr. Saunders." Her oyster-colored eyes flicked to Jamie, who still stood with her face pressed close to David's bare chest. "I knew a lot went on in this town, but I never for a mo-ment thought you'd be a part of that kind of thing!"

"I'm not a party to anything, Emma," he said tiredly. "Now go to bed, please. Good night to you all," he said, and he bounded up the stairs, his brown and white pa-jama jacket flapping at the sudden rush of speed.

Jamie, her face burning, hurried past the housekeeper to her own room. *That's done it,* she thought, sitting unhappily on the side of her bed. *The way gossip travels around this town, everybody will think David and I are secret lovers!*

She sat having late dinner with Thorne the following evening. She had hurried to one of the lesser Aspen shops to find a suitable dress and finally she'd found an emerald green silk that looked as if it came from the thirties. It was "dinkier," as her mother would have put it, than any other dress she'd ever worn. She had hesi-tated at first, seeing her firm, round young breasts peeking over the green material, but then she had real-ized she liked this new look of herself—it was mysteri-ous and worldly and yes, even chic—something which Aspen adored.

"You've got men drooling over you, do you know that?" Thorne poured more wine into her glass. They sat at a wall table at one of the most expensive moun-tainside restaurants in, or rather out, of town. "I'm not sure if I should take you to Cassie's party or not."

"So far, the parties around here get a very low rating from me," she told him, smiling. "At the last one I went to, nobody seemed to be having a very good time."

"Especially David." He drained his glass. His tanned, handsome face looked slightly flushed. "He's very fond of you, isn't he?"

"I suppose so, yes." She felt her heart give a little catch. It was very possible that Thorne had heard the gossip that Jamie felt certain David's housekeeper would have started by this time.

"He's actually a very hard man to dislike," Thorne said quietly, "even though he probably wishes I'd disintegrate over there on Silverlode."

Her heart went cold. "Don't say that! I don't think that's—funny," she said in a voice that nearly trembled. "David wouldn't wish you or anyone harm—he's a good, kind, decent—"

"Skip the last part," Thorne said, and for a second his eyes met hers. She saw accusation there; she was certain that was what she was seeing in those suddenly cold, vividly blue eyes.

"So you've heard the story. You have heard it, haven't you? All about how I was caught in David Saunders' arms—"

"I've heard," Thorne said easily, "but I don't believe it. Now drink your wine because it's far better to have a glow on when you go to one of Cassie's terrible parties."

She didn't like the wine; it made her feel heady and reckless, but she found herself drinking it anyway.

The party was, she realized later, very much like the one at Rhonda Miles' had been—crowded, with stale cigarette smoke and lovely china and silverware and hot, marvelously cooked food. There were women who wore practically no tops to their dresses and there were young men who seemed bored by those same women. When they were introduced to Jamie, the reaction was immediate—they clustered around her, while Thorne sat at the bar watching, smiling at her from time to time as more and more men wandered her way. It was as if they shared some delightful kind of joke between them, a secret of some sort.

"Is he the one, or is it the other one?" Jamie recognized the voice of the newspaperwoman they'd run into at the disco. Her hard eyes were staring at Thorne, there at the bar. "I still haven't been able to figure out whose girl you are, Jamie. Maybe that's why I haven't printed that item I got firsthand before breakfast this morning." She smiled. "It concerns you and David Saunders. My source said you were caught on the way to his bedroom, and that he wore the pajamas Rhonda Miles gave him." She pushed back her silver-streaked hair. "Rhonda will be furious about that. She's in love with him, you know."

"No, I didn't know that."

"I haven't been able to quote her on it because she won't admit it. There's that horribly rich prince from Saudi Arabia; he's just bought a house here. Anyway, dearest, I wanted to tell you what a clever girl I think you are—" She moved away, into the crowd.

"Don't talk to that witch," the young man who'd gone to get coffee for Jamie said. "We all loathe her and we're all scared to death of her, so she's always around. She was the first to announce my parents' divorce in her column." He handed the cup to Jamie. "Of course, it isn't every day that a sixty-year-old man divorces in order to marry a seventeen-year-old country and western singer, but that's exactly what my old man did. Would you like a sandwich?"

She found herself looking at this man, Peter, his name was, through the haze of smoke. He was young, a bit older than she was probably. He was tall and good-looking, with dark, nicely styled hair and friendly, mild gray eyes. He seemed very anxious to please her and he smoked constantly, his hands moving, his voice a little loud.

She was sorry for him, and, in a strange way, sorry for a lot of them. Never mind the money part; the fact was, this young man had been raised by a father who had abandoned his family out of lust for a very young girl. Her own father—thinking of him warmed her like a sweet drink. She saw him smiling, talking, gentle, good, loving. A rock.

She had been far luckier as a child than most of these people. She finally managed to excuse herself and walk over to Thorne.

"Do you think we could leave, please?"

His blue eyes seemed unusually bright. "Leave? The party's just got going." Someone bumped into him, a fattish girl in a black, backless dress. "That's the way Cassie's parties are."

"I really don't want to stay, Thorne."

He hardly seemed to hear her. "Tonight's the night two of my buddies plan to build a snowman and put a giant jug in his hand. Then, they're going to fill it with booze and see who can—" He stopped talking as Jamie walked away. "Wait a minute!" He looked down at her. "All I'm saying is that it's going to be a crazy party and let's stay." He took a sip of his drink. "That's nothing to walk out on me for, is it?"

She felt miserable, bewildered, as he seemed to make her feel so often. She suddenly had the insane wish not to be here at all, in this room, with these noisy, silly people, but to be somewhere else, someplace that did not include Thorne Gundersen's disturbing presence. His way of making her feel high with happiness and suddenly miserable and somehow angry was beginning to spoil everything.

"I'm not walking out," she said quietly. "I'm just saying I don't happen to like this party and I'd like to leave."

"You didn't even know these people until two or so nights ago, Jamie. Now you're setting yourself up as judge and jury. Did you get that nasty attitude all by yourself or did David Saunders teach it to you?"

She felt her eyes widen in a kind of stunned anger.

"Listen," he said quickly, "Jamie—I'm sorry. Listen, I didn't mean—"

But she had walked quickly away from him, through the crowd, out to the foyer where coats had been hung or tossed on chairs. There were expensive furs everywhere; Jamie looked for her wool plaid coat but didn't see it.

"I thought you'd blunder on out into the snow," Thorne said quietly from behind her. "You know——the wounded maiden going out into the blizzard because she got her feelings hurt."

She was unreasonably angry. "Don't bother to take me back to David's because I intend to call a cab just as soon as I find my coat."

He watched her as she lifted minks and seal and other furs, looked through what hung in the wide front closet, and finally found her own little coat under a table.

"I'm not letting you leave, you know." He was still looking at her, a small smile on his face. He seemed calm and almost pleased.

"And I'm not letting you keep me here." Her voice was firm and laced with the anger she was feeling. Somewhere behind her eyes, tears had formed, tears of frustration and self-rage. Why should she care so much for a man who treated her badly at times?

"Then we'll both leave." He put her coat around her shoulders. "I think," he said, ushering her out the front door, "it's time we came to some sort of understanding."

She was driving; it seemed strange to her, handling that sleek, powerful little car, but Thorne had asked her to, after they left the party.

"Where? Where do you want me to take us?"

He had settled himself in the seat beside her, long legs stuck out in front of himself, arms folded, head against the back of the seat.

"Up the mountain. As far up as the road goes."

She looked upward, feeling a sudden sense of fear. But the sense of hurt in her was still there, stronger than

caution, so she shoved the car into gear; it sprang forward like a shot and began the winding trail.

"You're an excellent driver," he shout finally, from
beside her. "You know this road?"

She glanced at him. He didn't seem at all afraid, and
the strange thing was—neither did she. She drove at a
reckless speed, drove until the feelings had left her, the
bad feelings, and she felt at last, roaring up that mountain road in his car, a deep sense of kinship with him, a
kind of bond.

His hand covered her small one, where it rested on
the gearshift.

"The road ends up there."

She nodded, beginning to slow the car. They came to
a stop at the barricade and suddenly, she turn to him,
without a word between them, they kissed deeply, ach-
ingly their hearts pounding against each other in that
very rare moment.

"Okay," he said finally, his mouth warm against her
ear, "I know I've given you a rough time. I know I've
no right to a girl like you. But I'm asking you to be my
girl, Jamie."

She nodded, head against his shoulder. Then she
raised her face and he began kissing her once again. It
had begun snowing again; flakes swirled around the tiny
car. And from its ancient place beyond them, the
treacherous Ajax seemed to be watching.

Jamie pulled away from his arms. How many days
left until that mountain tried to claim him?

David came into the kitchen ten minutes before his
usual time. It was very early; outside, it was as dark as
the night before.

"Well," he said, somewhat coldly, "I didn't expect to
see you here this morning. I thought sure you'd want to
sleep late."

"I've been up for over an hour," she said cheerfully,
mixing batter for pancakes. "Did you sleep well?"

He sat grouchily down at the table. "What're you doing there?"

"Making flapjacks for your breakfast," she said sweetly.

"Well, I can't eat that kind of stuff early in the morning." He sipped at his instant coffee. "Clogs my brain."

"All right, then; I'll eat some and fix you dry toast."

"I'm not an invalid, Jamie. And I'm not a hundred and twelve, so kindly stop treating me that way."

She began making coffee in the battered old pot. "I'm sure you aren't old, David. As a matter of fact, I heard last night that you're secretly in love."

His eyes narrowed. "It had to be Lydia Markin," he said. "She's the only one who would hand out such an absurd lie about me. I suppose you ran into the famous queen of the tabloids at that party your new boyfriend took you to?"

Jamie didn't answer him. He was very clearly in a vile temper about something and it wouldn't do a bit of good to press him for civilized conversation. She knew him quite well.

"I might try just one pancake," he said finally, as Jamie poured thick golden syrup over her plate of steaming, thickly stacked pancakes. "A small one."

She smiled at him. "I'll make it small enough," she said, "so that it doesn't clog your brain."

It was only a question of time before he was once again her charming, brilliant writer-benefactor, handing her pages of crisp dialogue and biting satire. They finished work early, soon after lunch. Since the housekeeper's intial session of gossiping, there had been no more of it, so far as Jamie knew. In fact, Emma went around looking guilty, serving an especially nice lunch to Jamie and David, as if to make up for things.

"She doesn't think we're lovers anymore," Jamie said, biting into the delicious hot apple pie.

"Would that guilt could make such good cooks of us all," David said, testing his delicate fish. "Actually, I'm very surprised that Lydia didn't mention that tidbit about me in pajamas and you with your arms around me in one of her rag papers."

"She said something about it. I expect she will say something nasty about me one day. She doesn't seem to like people very well."

"Then why would you believe her when she told you I'm secretly in love? Pass the butter, please."

"With my cooking and Emma's cooking, you're going to get very fat, David." Her voice was light and teasing.

"No chance. My wife was a marvelous cook and she used to make me fantastic things to eat. She cooked all over the world for me. She'd take a little portable hot plate along and when we were in, say, Paris—she'd go to the market and buy fresh stuff and come back to the hotel suite and cook." His eyes looked warm as he spoke. "Finally, we began renting flats, even if I only had to talk to a publisher for an hour; we'd take a flat for a month and then Margo would start playing house. She was like a child in a lot of ways."

"David," Jamie asked carefully, "are you sure you'll never marry again?"

"Are you proposing to me by any chance?"

Her face colored. "Of course not. It's only that—you very obviously need someone."

"I'm doing fine, thank you. Or I was, briefly, until you took up with your playboy ski friend."

Jamie let her breath out. "I've been waiting all day for you to get into a good mood and I'm not sure you're in one yet." She looked at him. "Are you?"

"Of course not. You ought to know by now that I'm never in a totally good mood; meanness and sarcasm are always lurking there behind the surface." He grinned. "What was it you wanted to ask me? Is it about your ski friend?"

"I wish you'd stop calling him that." She moved uncomfortably in the chair.

"All right, then—boyfriend. Now what?"

"It's only that I—I want you to understand that—that Thorne and I have an understanding. A sort of understanding, I guess you'd call it. We—made a sort of pact—"

"That sounds like a lot of rubbish. What sort of pact? Is he trying some sexual-fantasy-come-to-life trick on you?" His eyes were angry behind his glasses.

"Of course not! It's—simply that Thorne doesn't believe in talking about the past very much. It bores him. He told me that last night." She looked at her plate. "He also told me I've set myself up as judge and jury in the case of his friends. And he's right, David." She looked at him. "He's absolutely right. I guess I—caught that feeling from you. Oh," she said quickly, "it isn't that I'm blaming you, because I'm not. That wouldn't be fair. I'm saying that—it might be all right for you to do that; you're a writer and it's your business to make judgments, I suppose. But I was wrong to—to want to leave those parties almost as soon as I got there."

He was looking at her in the most peculiar way. Finally, he got up from the table and went over to the window. It had stopped snowing; a group of children just out of morning kindergarten stopped to wave at him. David waved back, then turned to face Jamie.

"You're caught up in it already," he said quietly. "You don't know it yet, but you are."

"I'm not—caught up in anything—"

"Yes, you are. Somehow, you aren't seeing straight any longer. One moment, you were able to see the insanity of the way they live, and suddenly, it all seems just fine to you. I'm sure you can thank your—boyfriend—for your newly moronic viewpoint."

Jamie stood up. She had thought David might be difficult, when she told him of her relationship with Thorne, when she told him that now, for a while at least, she was Thorne's girl, his love.

She had expected some display of outrage, but instead David stood there very quietly, almost sadly.

"I suppose you'll refuse to go to Jamaica with me, too. Now that you've got yourself tied down—"

"I'm not tied down!" She rang for Emma to clear the

trays; that was usually a signal that her time with David had more or less ended for the day. Lunch trays, tea trays cleared out, papers neatly stacked, sometimes a final cup of spiced tea with him; then, the fire was put out for the day, unless, of course, she or David planned to stay in and use the study to read. Neither of them had done that lately; she'd hear his Jag drive up in the very early hours of the morning. Sometimes, she herself got in very late, or very early in the morning, but David seemed to be making a habit of late homecomings.

"You can forget Jamaica," he said as she stood stacking manuscript papers on her desk, preparing to leave the room, end the workday and, of course, avoid further discussion of her relationship with Thorne. "I know you'll refuse to go and I'm not sure I can do the book without you. It's as simple as that."

She felt suddenly ashamed of herself. This man, this good, kind, grieving man needed her.

"Can't we stay on here and work on your book, David? I promise I won't cause you any more worry." She leaned over to pick up a sheet of copy paper that had fluttered to the floor. At the same time David came quickly across the room and bent to retrieve it. They were suddenly very close, there on the floor.

"We'll stay here," he said gently. "And if he hurts you—I swear I'll kill him!"

It wasn't until she was upstairs soaking in the tub, in the pretty, newly decorated bath connected to her bedroom, that Jamie remembered something important: she had meant to ask David about Rhonda, to get him to talk about that sultry, spoiled but very charming young woman.

As she buttoned the gold sweater she'd chosen to wear over warm slacks, the thought came clearly into her mind: *Am I trying to bring David around to talking about his true feelings for Rhonda so that I don't have to examine my own real feelings for Thorne?*

Thirty minutes later, in the hallway, standing in Thorne's strong arms in the dim light, her mouth yielding under his, gone trembling and soft under his, she forgot the nagging little worry that was always there, hiding, inside her mind.

"You smell like some kind of lovely flowers," he said, his mouth against her hair. "We could skip the dinner party at Friday's and go to my house early—"

She had promised herself to draw the line. It had something to do with what David had warned her about, something to do with survival, but she wasn't sure what.

"I think we'd better go to Friday's."

He sighed. "Okay. I'm going to have to be a good boy, even if I was awake half the night thinking about you."

The dinner party at the popular gathering spot was, as Jamie had expected, extremely noisy and brawlsome. The parties given in owned, leased or rented-for-the-weekend houses were subdued to some degree by the fact that they were held in somebody's *house*. Here, it was a bar, a posh disco-type place with a long bar and a dance floor and eerie lights. The dinner was being given by a young married couple who studiously avoided getting close to each other during the entire evening.

Later, in the parking lot, heading for a coffeehouse down the street along with Thorne and ten or so merry, slightly drunk friends, Jamie saw the party's hostess in a car with a man who wasn't her husband. The man kissed her and slid the straps of her dress down from her shoulders.

"You look upset," Thorne told her, as they pushed their way through the noisy crowd at the coffeehouse. "Are you okay?"

She nodded. It seemed to her that it was impossible to talk in this place; it was all a blur of sweatered, smiling, beautiful-looking people, moving from table to table, kissing, hugging, chatting. They were probably the richest, most spoiled generation in history, or at least one of them. They had all inherited their money, and although they were all well-educated, none of them seemed to Jamie to be one-hundredth as interesting as David Saunders.

"At least nobody minds if I kiss you here," Thorne said, as mugs of coffee and doughnuts were placed before them. He leaned toward her, his eyes warm—partly, she suspected, from the wine and brandy he'd had earlier. "There's another party starting in a while," he said softly, "breakfast and beds, if anybody's interested." He kissed her mouth gently. "Is anybody?"

"Not tonight. I have to be in David's kitchen very early, for what he calls our prework conference."

He hadn't heard her; the band was too noisy. So they sat holding hands, not talking; Jamie smiled up into some stranger's face now and again, as people stopped to hug or kiss Thorne or shake his hand.

Be happy, she told herself, as the music seemed to get louder and more and more women stopped by to give the grinning Thorne deep, provocative kisses. Be happy; this is what you've always wanted—a magnificent man, exciting parties and interesting friends!

She could almost hear David's sarcastic voice: *"What friends?"*

CHAPTER VII

She was not sleeping well at all. Her life had resumed a normal facade; she was always in the kitchen moments before David, making coffee, teasing him, talking about his book, being cheerful and, she hoped, sounding very sane and sensible and happy.

But he wasn't fooled. Why had she even for a moment thought that she could fool David? He knew her, and in a way, she knew and understood him as he did her. So it was only a question of time before he faced her with the truth: she was not happy.

When David would come into the kitchen and have his breakfast, he said very little. He ate, but not with the heartiness he'd once had, and when it was time to begin work, he typed with a fury, sitting across the room from her, banging away on his typewriter.

"It's not very good, is it?" he asked her one evening. He got up from his desk, looking rather thin and weary. "Something seems to have gone wrong."

"David—"

He went to the window; his wide, rather bony shoulders seemed slumped. "I'm sure you know what I'm talking about. You've become my severest—and best—critic." He looked hard at her. "Well, Jamie, I'm right, am I not? My novel has become a burden to me. It's going along, but the magic isn't there anymore. The truth is, my dear, I'm spending all my energy worrying over you and what's to become of you." He seemed to hesitate. "What if he dies on that mountain? What will you do then?"

"I don't think about that." She folded her hands, there at her desk. She'd slept badly, gotten only four hours' rest and probably only minutes of actual sleep, and now, at the beginning of a long day, she already felt tired and edgy.

"Do you realize that every hostess in Aspen is trying to get in touch with you?"

"No," Jamie said, surprised, "I didn't know that. There've been no calls or messages—"

"I'm afraid there have," he said unabashedly. "I simply didn't give them to you. In my opinion, you're going to many too many social disgraces right now. If I start telling you all the people who want you to drop by and say hello—and bring Thorne, naturally—I'd never get my book typed. You'd spend all your time being the belle of the Beautiful People. Their pet, their darling for this season. They love finding a pet, you know. Last year it was an artist, the year before that a clever fellow who painted fake masterpieces and sold them at outrageous prices. He cheated them but they adored him anyway. They're after you, Jamie, like hunters after the hunted. And that is why I can't stop worrying."

"I'd like very much for you to stop worrying about me. I know you don't approve of my—friendship with Thorne and I'm sorry about that." She decided to go ahead and say it: "Please don't ask me not to see him anymore, because I've no intention of listening if you do."

"Does he love you?" It was a direct question; his eyes were steady and dark behind his glasses. "Has he told you he does?"

"That's really none of your business!" She had not meant to sound so harsh; sometimes David could be very much like a spoiled, dependent child, always telling her how much he needed her and then behaving in a very naughty way.

"Now I've got you angry with me," he said, shaking his head. "Come on; let's get to work. Maybe this pea brain of mine will come up with some great idea to make you happy again."

Happy *again?* What about—what about her happiness with Thorne?

She concentrated on her work for the next four and a half hours, there in David's study. He was across the room at his typewriter only for half the morning or less. Once, as she glanced out the window, weary of the sound of the new electric typewriter, she saw David crossing the street, dodging traffic, apparently in a great hurry.

She went back to work. She hadn't read this chapter of his book yet and she found that, although it was fiction and names were changed, the people in it sometimes were very clearly those she had spoken to or danced with or sat with the night before at some party Thorne had taken her to. The parties were endless; they went on at odd hours of the day and all night, every night. For a break from them, people skied or sat around the big, comfortable but always crowded Lodge, or they bunched into bars or coffeehouses, looking for someone to tell them where the best party going was.

Around noon, she stood up to stretch and saw David coming hurriedly around the corner. He checked his watch, came up onto the porch and stomped his feet to get snow off. Then he came inside and began yelling for Jamie.

"Here I am! David—what on earth is—"

"I was afraid you'd finished up early and left." He glanced at the housekeeper who was looking at him as if he'd lost his mind. "It's perfectly all right, Emma. I'm taking my secretary on a picnic, so I wonder if you'd mind putting whatever you've fixed for us in a box or something."

"A picnic! David, it's supposed to snow today!" That was so; Thorne had told her he'd be on the slopes early, getting up very early to practice-run. He was to call her at five, something about a cocktail party at someone's house.

"Snow? Put in a thermos of soup, please, Emma. And maybe some brandy. Get your coat, Jamie, we're leaving."

"But—"

He reached into the front closet and took out a plastic clothes-bag, reaching into it. "Here—this was Margo's. It's warmer than animal fur; she'd never wear that. Put it on and come and see what's waiting in front."

For an instant Jamie felt hesitant about putting on the dead woman's coat, but the feeling quickly passed. It was indeed a lovely sort of garment, soft and light but wonderfully cozy and warm. There was a hood; David quickly flipped it up and tied it beneath her chin as if she were a child.

"Come along; I have to pay by the hour, you know."

"What?"

"He told me we could keep her as long as we want but it's by the hour. If you like it and we don't freeze, we can go all the way out to a place I think you'll like, for dinner."

She had stepped out the door, warmly bound by the jacket and hood, and now she stared out to the street. There was a horse and buggy there, waiting, tied to a young tree.

"Like it?"

"David, I'm not sure I—"

"Of course you can. He'll be on the mountain all day anyway, most likely. There isn't that much time before the big day, is there? I promise I'll have you back early enough for him to keep you out half the night. Okay?" She couldn't refuse. Emma handed David a rather large box and a very large thermos of homemade soup, and waved as David, settled on the driver's side, urged the horse to start walking.

"Emma's a terrible liar," David said. "She never makes her own soup. It's always out of a can." He smiled at Jamie, there beside him on the seat. "Warm enough?"

She saw worry and something that was so much concern it could have been love in his eyes. Love—she didn't want that from this man. But there was something she did want, and that was a little wisdom.

She was beginning to feel that her feeling for Thorne was some kind of wild mistake, that it shouldn't have happened. It was a terrible thing to admit, but there were moments, at a party or watching women and young girls crowd around him, that she had a certain feeling of despair inside her, the feeling that, if she'd never met him, her life could have been smooth, happy, with no wild ups and no plunging downs.

So it felt good, sitting beside David, knowing that, no matter what happened, no matter what was said, it wouldn't change their friendship. In a way, perhaps she needed David as much as he said he needed her.

There was snow on the ground and on the trees; it was like a ride into a crystal-white place she'd never been before. The jacket and lap robes kept her quite warm; David had reached into Margo's coat and pulled out a pair of small, warm mittens that easily fit Jamie's hands. Oddly enough, she did not feel ill at ease about the mittens or coat; she had enjoyed listening to David speak of Margo. He didn't do it often, but Jamie felt certain it had been a beautiful love story and that someday he would write about it.

His glasses steamed up from the cold, finally, so they pulled off the pretty, winding back road and he uncorked the thermos.

"Here. You have the soup and I'll have the brandy."

"Not yet. David—it was very nice of you to do this."

"Good. I was afraid I might have to bring you kicking and hollering." He poured himself a tiny sip of brandy into the top of the flask. "I have something to tell you, you see. It's got to do with loving other people. I don't think you understand what I'm talking about and I mean to see that you do."

Yes, she was ready to talk about that. Because she was certain that she was in love with Thorne, and nearly certain that he loved her.

Perhaps David could help her discover why this fact made her uneasy, even unhappy sometimes.

They rode for the better part of an hour. There was a roadside lodge about thirty minutes out, and they warmed their feet there and watched a three-year-old boy deftly put on his skis.

"Starting early," David said, helping her into the buggy once more. "Come on—the horse is getting a bit cold, I think."

She mentioned the child over cocktails at one of David's favorite places, an old inn at the end of a narrow, snowy road.

"I wonder if that little boy will go on with it."

"The one putting on skis? Yes," David told her, "I thought that would ring a bell somewhere inside your head." He reached over and covered her hand with his. He still wore his wedding ring. "You're afraid for him, aren't you?"

She knew he was talking not about the child but about Thorne. Out the far window, one could see Ajax. They had spent all those hours, riding in the buggy, stopping to get warm, stopping for tea, now they were here, and they were both chilled and tired, and there it was, there was the mountain, still there, as huge as ever, watching her.

There was no running away from it. Or from the fact that, in a matter of days—nine to be exact—Thorne would be trying to ski down the far face of it, all the way down. And nobody had ever done that, including her cousin.

"Aren't you, Jamie?"

"Yes," she said softly. "Of course I'm afraid for him. But I can't stop him. Nobody could do that."

"I might be able to."

She looked at him. She knew the look; David had some plan in mind. It was the same look his face had when he was planning a chapter, thinking about a character. He had some plan in mind.

"You think you can convince Thorne not to ski Silverlode? I thought you were, when you come right down to it, a realist, David."

"I am." He let go her hand, searching for his pipe. "It's all part of a kind of planned hoopla that basically makes a lot of people in town very rich. Just having Thorne Gundersen in the general area makes them generally rich. Groupies flock here to get a look at him. Parents fly here to bring groupie kids home, but not until they've hung around long enough——probably until after Thorne tries to ski Silverlode Run——to spend more money than the average man makes in six months. And perhaps more importantly——" He was lighting his pipe, puffing away furiously, looking at her through the blue smoke, "the Beautiful People want him to ski Ajax. They want a hero, even if it's soon going to be a dead one."

She put her glass down very quickly. "Thorne is—more capable than my cousin was. He wouldn't try it if he didn't feel he could make it. Not to please his friends, or groupies or anyone."

"Jamie," David said gently, "before you can help him, you're going to have to try to understand him. And you don't, you know. That's what's wrong; that's what's missing. He kisses you very well; it's probably going to end up in very wonderful sex, possibly before he tries Silverlode, but the point is——the two of you communicate about as well as Rhonda and I do. We aren't bitter enemies; in fact, from time to time we've been physical lovers. I'm not being ungentlemanly——everyone here knows she's spent nights here, or else I haven't rushed directly home after one of her crazy parties. But what I'm saying is simply that, although in a way I find Rhonda very interesting and even exciting, we never talk about anything real." He signaled the waiter. "Let's go and sit by the fireplace while they fix our dinner, Jamie. They've a very pleasant, private dining room in the back. Would you like to eat in there?"

It was a charming room, very old; it had been some

kind of back bedroom in the old house during the days when Aspen was rawly young. It had been one of the first houses in town, built soon after the town had been named by a shrewd man who had sometimes been called a low-down claim jumper: Clark Wheeler. He'd called it Aspen, because of the trees in the area. The miners had killed a lot of them, but they were still plentiful, there on the mountains, lining the roads.

"A man named Deerjack built this house," David told Jamie, settling himself beside her on the low couch in front of the fireplace. The door to the room had been left discreetly open, but all the same, the room seemed very private. "He made his money mining silver. They say he promised his wife a fine house and built this one for her. Unfortunately, he was killed in one of the mines before they moved in here. So she didn't move in either—she went back East to Philadelphia. So you see, if it hadn't been for his ambition—"

"Are you trying to tell me something, David?"

"Of course. But it isn't something you don't know right now. Thorne hasn't a chance in the wind of surviving that ski run. But he knows that too. That's what I don't understand."

Suddenly Jamie thought she could hear the wind outside, the cold wind that sometimes rattled windows and seemed to knock on doors, like a ghost or perhaps like some angel come to call. *The angel of death.*

"You're wrong, David," she said quietly, "Thorne wouldn't try unless he was confident—"

"Stop kidding yourself, Jamie! Listen," he said earnestly, bending toward her in front of the warm fire, his face worried. "I talk to people, on the phone, in a bar. I'm not always behind that desk working, as you may or may not have noticed. And the word is that Thorne Gundersen is as good as dead!"

She stared at him, slow horror creeping over her. It was possible; it was entirely possible that he wasn't lying, or trying to frighten her into making a move. David didn't want to manipulate her or anyone; that was one of the things he always put down in his books: loss of personal freedom, selfish manipulation—he hated those things and said so.

"We've got to stop him," she said finally. "David—if anyone can talk to him, you can!"

He leaned back in his chair. "Think it'll do any good? You haven't known him long but I'm sure you know him better than that."

Her hand had begun trembling on the glass. "Is this what you've been wanting to talk to me about?"

"Partly. I also wanted you to understand something about loving someone. I'm not sure you're past the dating stage with Thorne. And I'm not at all sure it isn't the fascination of who he is that's charming you—not the man himself."

"David, I don't think—"

"Of course you don't. Not about what you should be thinking about, anyway. That, little girl, is why I've gone to the trouble of freezing my feet to come all the way out here in that infernal, cold buggy—not just because it's quaint but to give you a chance to get away from Gundersen and do some clear thinking. Mountain air," he said, "is supposed to be good for that."

She looked at him. There was no doubting the kindness and deep concern in his eyes. And he was right, of course; he was only saying something outright that she had felt all along. It was wild insanity for Thorne to try to make it down Silverlode. Silverlode was one of those trails that wasn't meant to be conquered.

"You're saying that by allowing myself to be in love with Thorne, I'm setting myself up for a very bad time if he doesn't make it." He didn't answer her, but she knew, of course, that was what David had been talking about. "Well, then, what should I do?" *Walk to the phone,* she told herself. *Call Thorne and tell him either to forget Silverlode or else forget me!*

"Two possible answers, I'd say. Let's order dinner and we'll discuss them." He smiled at her. "I really think you're going to like one of them very much."

She tried to eat, to please David, but it was very difficult. He had a way of getting through to the truth, like the little child in the fable about the naked king. Now, now that she was forced to face the distinct possibility that, very soon now, she might be forced to go through the pain of loss she'd suffered when her cousin had died.

"Should I say it?" She put down her napkin. "I wish I'd never met him."

"Good," David said heartily. "That's a healthy beginning. Eat your salad and I'll tell you what I have in mind."

"I'm not going to Jamaica, if that's what you mean."

"I've no intention of trying to take you away from it all, Jamie. If you really think that, let me waste no time in telling you what seems to me to be the best possible solution to what we're both dreading—your friend's trip down the mountain on skis." He leaned closer to her. "We simply put a stop to it. To the exhibition."

"But—how could we—"

"We ban it. We get people to sign a paper and we take it wherever we need to so nobody will ever get killed on that mountain again—at least not for the purposes of making money. Did you ever stop to think what Thorne's being paid to take that chance?"

Would he, was it possible that he would risk his life for money? She threw aside that thought almost immediately. Thorne didn't need money; his father had left him a fortune. Besides, he seemed to have a peculiar dislike for material things—the lovely mountainside house was rented, so was the furniture. His car had been expensive at one time, but now it was rather old and somewhat battered-looking.

Skiing was the only thing that really seemed to matter to him.

"If he loved me," she said quietly, "and I asked him not to, then the problem would be solved, wouldn't it?" She reached for her scarf. "David, I'd like to leave now. I'd like to get back so I can talk to Thorne."

"And if that doesn't work?"

"If that doesn't work, you can get your petition ready."

It was dusk when they got back. David let her out at the corner, saying he was going to take the horse and rig back to its owner and pay him. She walked through the gathering darkness to the house, then stopped.

Thorne's little car was parked in front. There was a light on in the living room, and as she went into the hallway, she saw Thorne sprawled in one of the big chairs.

"I was afraid you weren't coming back," he said, standing up to greet her. "The housekeeper invited me in. We've just got time to get over there to the party."

She began taking off her things. "I'm not going, Thorne."

He frowned. "Something wrong?"

"Yes—a lot of things. I suppose we could begin with Silverlode."

"I wondered when you'd get around to that. Look— let's forget the stupid party. Let's go to my place instead."

She shook her head. "I'm tired and cold and I need some time to think. Not tonight, Thorne."

He shrugged. "Even a local hero gets turned down sometimes."

"Is that what you want to be? The local hero?" There was a cool edge to her tone.

He was silent for a second. "Isn't that what you see me as?"

His words stunned her. David had implied nearly the same thing earlier—that her feelings were imagined, based on glamour and the idea of danger and excitement.

"Good night," she said unsteadily, and she fled up the stairs to her room. Moments later, she heard Thorne's car start and drive away.

He had asked her to be his girl. And she had thought

that meant he loved her. But he had not told her that, and deep down there was some invisible door he held closed against her, some secret he kept that he would not share with her.

Perhaps, she thought suddenly, *he wants to die!*

And it was that thought, that wild guess, that caused her to dial Thorne's number at quarter-past four the following morning.

He sounded somewhat foggy.

"I called to tell you I'm sorry," she said. "It wasn't that I didn't want to talk—"

"Talking seems to get us in a lot of trouble. Why don't we try sign language instead?"

It was good to hear his voice warming, beginning to tease her. It made her fear ease a little. Perhaps she would be able to talk some sense into him after all. Perhaps he really did care enough about her to listen.

"Are you going out to practice-run this morning, Thorne?"

"I planned to sleep in this morning, unless you'd like to come over and cook my breakfast."

"I have to go to work. I want to talk to you—"

"I thought we agreed not to do that."

She heard the banging sound of David, downstairs in the kitchen. He was up very early.

"Then," she said slowly, "I guess I shouldn't see you again." Her own words surprised her. "Because I'm tired of all the parties and the people who call here to try to get me to drag you off to some party they're giving. I'm tired of—of dreading what you're going to do. I should know better than a lot of people—they wanted my cousin to become their darling, too, but he didn't."

"Maybe he should have," Thorne said dryly. "There's nothing particularly wrong with the eat, drink and be merry life-style, Jamie. Except that people don't want to get up early."

From downstairs came the loud sound of a clattering pan and then David's loud *"Damn!"*

"I have to go, Thorne. I just wanted you to know I

wasn't avoiding you last night. And I'm willing to talk about us. If," she said quietly, "there really is an Us."

She hung up, feeling strangely disappointed. Thorne would call her or come by, she felt certain, and yet she felt so unsure of his real feelings that even if he did call and want to see her, nothing would change most likely.

She found David in the kitchen, reading over some pages and drinking coffee.

"It's instant," he told her. "I gave up after I dropped the soup pot on my foot when I was looking for Emma's coffeepot."

"I'll fix you something to eat," she told him.

Jamie could feel him watching her as she moved about the kitchen. It was perhaps the least attractive room in the old house, and yet the nicest. For all her faults, Emma seemed capable of making any place where her employer lived cozy and comfortable, and this house was no exception.

"Well?"

"Well, what?" She got out a cup and saucer from the cupboard.

"I heard you up and about early, so I suppose you've called him. Did you?"

Her face flushed. "Yes, as a matter of fact I did."

"And?"

"He doesn't—want to talk. He said something about knowing that sooner or later I'd get upset about Silverlode."

David began gathering up his papers. "Remember what I told you: if you can't talk him into giving up on this suicide scheme, I'll try to stop him legally. But there isn't much time."

Time went very slowly that day. She'd had only snatches of sleep the night before; she was nervous and time seemed to crawl by as she typed. David worked until only about ten that morning; he said he had business to take care of and left before their usual shared lunch.

Emma surprised Jamie when she tapped on the door and then came in without the usual lunch tray.

"It's my day off," she announced. "There's plenty to eat."

"Oh—thank you, Emma. Please don't let me spoil your day—I'll be fine."

"You won't." She looked at Jamie with unfriendly eyes. "Someone is waiting to see you. I told her I'd see if you could break away from your work."

"Her?"

"Rhonda Miles. She's in the living room."

It would seem that Rhonda was bolder than any of the others. She came herself instead of phoning to ask Jamie to bring Thorne to some party!

Rhonda sat in David's favorite chair, looking stunning. Her coppery hair was pulled back from her lovely face, and as always she wore clothes that were casual, yet chic and expensive-looking.

"Actually," she said, "I came to see David."

"He's gone to town," Jamie told her. "I'll be glad to—"

"Do you mind if I stay a moment?"

"Of course not." Jamie sat in a chair opposite Rhonda, feeling decidedly uncomfortable. Would you like something? Emma's leaving, but I can—"

"No, thank you. All I really want is to ask you something." She was reaching through her large purse; she came up with a cigarette and lit it. *She's uncomfortable, being near me,* Jamie thought. *More so than I am here with her.*

Rhonda looked at her steadily through the haze of smoke; her gray-silver eyes were decidedly unfriendly.

"I came here to ask David if he'd like to go to Vegas with a party of people. It's to be a sort of birthday party for him."

"But you don't need me to—"

"I'm sure he wouldn't want to come without you. I thought I might persuade you to talk to him. It might be good for him to get away." She looked away from Jamie. "I think it's time to see if he's really over Margo."

You mean, thought Jamie, *you want to see if he might by any chance be in love with you!*

And suddenly she felt very sorry for this beautiful young woman, who seemed to have it all, everything, all the gifts—youth, great beauty, uncountable money, a sleek car parked out in front. The chilly eyes were only masks; Jamie sensed a real feeling, and she recognized it, perhaps because she felt so uncertain about Thorne. Even beautiful, wealthy girls like this one could love a man and feel he really didn't care very much one way or the other.

Was that how Thorne felt about her?

"I'm afraid you'll have to ask David himself," Jamie told her, wishing this hadn't been put upon her. "He'll be back—"

"Are you in love with David by any chance?"

Jamie looked back at her evenly. "Mr. Saunders is my employer, nothing more."

"Because if you are, if you're only using Thorne as a means of making David Saunders notice you, let me tell you right here and now—it won't work. Oh, he might get excited about you because you've got him working again, but that will fade. He'll sell this book and people will pat him on the back and before long he'll settle into just the kind of life he wants—his life with Margo."

"Margo! But David's wife is—"

"Of course Margo's dead. But not for David. He may not talk about her a lot but you can bet he thinks of her most of the time. He'll never find anyone to replace his perfect wife." She ground out her cigarette. "You see, this way he doesn't have to bother to love anyone. And if he doesn't love, he won't get hurt."

"Miss Miles," Jamie said carefully, "don't you understand that it isn't up to me to change that? I'm not the one who loved David." She took a small breath, feeling she shouldn't say any more. "Are you sure you wouldn't like to help me scramble up some lunch?"

For a brief instant, the cold eyes wavered. There was

a quick, fleeting second when Jamie was sure Rhonda wanted to stay, to talk, perhaps even to confide in her.

"Thank you, no. But please tell David about the Vegas trip—I'm sure you can convince him he needs a few days off from his book." She picked up her purse. "Thorne's coming, of course. Hasn't he told you?"

"No." Jamie felt her heart start to beat harder. "He—didn't mention it."

"Someone should have warned you, dear." The silver eyes were ice. "When Thorne begins to tire of one of his girls, he lets her down ever so gently."

CHAPTER VIII

She had become as if she were two persons, the capable young secretary who expertly and carefully did her work for David, fixed his breakfast and sometimes his tea, and saved her more-than-generous salary, for the most part. David liked her; there was every reason to believe he'd want to keep her on, since they got along so well and he seemed pleased with her work.

So in a sense, her life could go along very smoothly—traveling with David, being his friend, not having to worry anymore about whether or not she should consider marrying him if he should ever ask her. She could and probably would remain single, should she make up her mind to stop being foolish over Thorne Gundersen.

Then, there was this other side of her, this new and very frightening side that showed itself when Rhonda made her nasty remark. Rhonda had left rather quickly after that, all to the good, since Jamie had stood there shaken and trying hard not to show what she couldn't help feeling.

David came back for lunch, peeking into the study where Jamie had gone back to her work.

"You don't spell very well, do you?"

He grinned. "I'm fixing lunch for us today. Omelets. I stopped in town and got some very nice squid."

She stood up, stretching. He looked unusually happy and confident.

"I've finished everything you left for me. And, oh, yes—you had a visitor."

"I'll be in the kitchen," he told her. "A visitor?"

"Miss Miles came by. She wants you to go to Las Vegas."

"Is she going?"

"Of course. She's planning the whole thing around your birthday." She picked up an apple from the kitchen table. "I didn't know your birthday was coming up. I'll have to hurry with your present."

"I'm reading your very sweet little mind," he told her, beginning to crack what seemed to Jamie to be an endless amount of eggs into a dish. "You're wondering how ancient I am and you're about to try to talk me into going to Vegas. Not, let me add, because you want to go yourself, but because you want me to spend some time with the red-haired Rhonda. Very transparent, my dear. Clear as a summer's day."

She looked at him. He had an uncanny way of knowing what she was thinking, or worrying about. And a very nice way of somehow making her feel that it was all going to be fine.

Even though she'd had a horrible dream the night before, a nightmare. It had only lasted a second, two or three at the most, but she'd seen someone from afar, looking down from some sort of very high place, and she'd seen Thorne, racing down Silverlode like a free bird, and then, she'd known he was going to fall, to go down like a wounded eagle, and she couldn't bear it so her dream blanked out.

"I'm going to talk to Thorne tonight," she told David. "I'm going to do what I can to stop him." She watched him as he cheerfully began beating the eggs. "David—you've something up your sleeve, haven't you?"

"I don't think you're going to have to worry much longer about your friend's going down Silverlode. I've been very busy this morning."

"David—what—"

"I'm going to stop him cold, that's what."

"But how?"

He smiled at her like a sly cat. "By virtue of my golden tongue."

"What?"

"I'm going to give a lecture, my dear." He flipped the omelet over and patted it gently. "I'm going to rent a hall and tell everybody in town that if Gundersen dies like all the others, his blood is going to be on their hands. Then, I'm going to tell them that I'm announcing the theme of my novel and my announcement is going to scare the hell out of them. Because I'm going to make every one of those people feel like a murderer."

He meant it. Up until now the theme of his book had been kept a secret from the press and his public, those loyal fans of his who always waited to read his novels, who adored the movies made of them and who looked upon him as a kind of brittle, brilliant jewel pointing an accusing finger at life. But now he was going to let the secret come out. Perfect timing, he told her.

She felt her heart lighten. Time was going to be on her side. If Thorne couldn't ski Silverlode, there might be time for him to consider giving it up entirely, finding another way of living his life altogether.

But before she could think about sharing that with him, she had to know if, as Rhonda had implied, she was only another one of the many, many girls Thorne had managed to have fall in love with him.

"There," David said after a while, "isn't it beautiful?"

It was, surprisingly. David's manner was so confident and cheerful that she couldn't help but feel he'd solved the problem of saving Thorne's life—for the time being, at least.

But the other problem still remained. What was his, Thorne's, real feeling for her?

Thorne called her at seven; his voice was contrite.

"It's a very nice night on the mountain," he told her. "Would you like to go and see?"

"Can we talk? Please? Will you listen to me and try to understand what I'm telling you?"

"I'll listen."

But he didn't say he'd do anything except what he'd been planning to do all along: make it down the killer Silverlode.

He took her into his arms as soon as she opened the front door for him.

"You're right about the parties. Let's forget all about them." He kissed her again. "Besides, I want to spend as much time alone with you as I can."

She looked into his eyes. "Before what, Thorne?"

It seemed to her that she'd hit target. He quickly got her out the front door, down to the curb and into his car. As they pulled away, Jamie thought she saw David watching from an upstairs window. She turned to Thorne.

"I'd like to walk someplace, if you don't mind."

The car shot forward. "Not here," he told her, his hand warmly finding hers. Jamie felt her heart race at his touch. "Let's go on up the mountain road."

It was beautiful: crystal-clear stars bright in a black sky, the mountains covered with snow, trees dressed in its whiteness. The moon was high and very bright, with just a part of its face hidden. Jamie leaned her head back and sighed.

"It's so beautiful here—whenever I think of going home I only have to walk down this road and look around me. The truth is, I'm not sure I ever want to leave, even though it's very hard to feel at home here."

He parked the car just off the road, on a small overlook that showed them majestic mountains and the twinkling lights from houses in town and outside. "I've never felt at home anyplace," he told her. "You get used to the feeling. Warm enough?"

"I'm fine." She snuggled under his arm. She felt so good with him, so *right* with him; it was as if she'd been fashioned to be just tall enough for this, to fit under his protective arm, to look up into his face; it was as if she'd been made for this man, her body proportioned to suit his.

They walked a long way, stopping once to break frozen, glittering ice off a nearby tree. When it began to get slick, they turned and walked back to the overlook and the car.

In the car, after starting it and turning on the heater, he turned to look at her. "Will you stay with me tonight, Jamie?"

Her breath caught in her throat. "I want to," she said steadily, "but first—I want to talk to you."

Oddly enough, she thought of the shattered glass, the glass that had been strewn about on the floor that time she was here, and then later, replaced. For some reason, she thought of that and the thought somehow bothered her.

"Thorne?" She sipped the drink he'd fixed her. Warming and syrupy sweet, with the alcohol buried somewhere in it. She decided not to finish it; she didn't want to be hazy about what she felt or said tonight. Not a bit of it.

"Mmmm." He was pulling the wide drapes that covered the window. "There; now you won't be upset by the mountain." He came over and sat on the couch beside her. "Now, that's better." He kissed her mouth lightly, lingeringly. "Isn't that better?"

Jamie gently pulled out of his arms. "I've come to ask you something." She took a small breath. "Please don't try Silverlode. Whatever thoughts you've been thinking about her—put them out of your mind. Because—because if you don't, she'll kill you!"

The starkness of her words got to him; his eyes, cleared of their passion, met hers.

"Is that what you want of me, Jamie? Just that? And then what?" He got up from the couch, his hands jammed into his pockets, his big shoulders hunched as if in rage. He went to the window and opened it, sliding back the glass so that the sharp, cold air came in. "That's the high, Jamie. That's the ultimate, the prize, right there. Better than a woman, better than ten thousand women, because she's timeless. She sits there century after century, seducing men, getting them to try to conquer her, but they never do." He was looking at Ajax, his eyes narrowed, squinting. "She's one hell of a lady," he said softly.

For Jamie, sitting there, beginning to get cold, it was the artless end of the evening, an evening that had begun so beautifully. She smiled as Thorn closed the glass and came back to be beside her. The mood of the moment was gone; there was no point now in asking him a question so blunt, so foolish as *Do you love me?* No point at all, since he had just shown her the great love of his life.

They listened to some music, ate some cheese someone in the cheese business had sent him (from Wisconsin) and ultimately danced, very closely, her face lightly touching the front of his ski sweater.

"Thorne?"

"Don't talk, just move."

She looked up at him. "When you said you've never felt at home anywhere, did you really mean that?"

"Of course. Rich kids seldom do, you know. It's part of the curse. My parents owned—let's see—seven—no, eight houses, not including that farmhouse in the vineyard I told you about. The odd thing is, I can't remember very much about any of them. Sometimes I'll recall the shape of a chair, or the way it looked outside when a door was open, but most of the time, it—simply seems as if I've never lived anywhere." He kissed her softly, the sweet wetness of their mouths clinging. "Unreal," he said.

Jamie struggled to stay in reality, instead of allowing herself to be carried along on that flight that would take her straight to the stars—

"I'm going to make coffee," she said suddenly, breaking away from him.

"Coffee? Now?"

"Of course." Jamie slid out of his arms. "We're going to spend the entire night talking."

That's exactly what they did, surprisingly. Around four, when the coffee no longer would work, with Thorne still sitting on the floor against the glass wall, his back to the mountains—Jamie dropped off to sleep.

The talk had been low-keyed, friendly, and although she'd dreaded it, afraid it might only be the question-answer kind of evening, it wasn't at all.

He had talked, for instance, of his mother: "I don't remember her very well. They were divorced and I was in school, in Paris. There was a telephone call from my father and I was put on a plane where all the hostesses were overly nice to me. I knew something was wrong, someplace. Women," he'd told her, "are usually very transparent about their feelings."

"Am I transparent?"

He'd smiled. "Not all of the time. I guess that's partly why I want to make love to you."

He had not wanted to talk about Ajax, however. He kept saying he wanted to make love to her and he told her wild stories about his childhood, where he'd lived with first one parent and summers, the other. When his mother was killed in a boat-sailing race off the coast of Palm Beach, he'd begun going to a series of expensive schools, from most of which he'd managed to get himself expelled. It was a now-familiar kind of story, the lonely child, shuttled from one country to another on jets, attending schools where he had to spend Christmas and other holidays because his father was A Very Busy Man, and the ultimate discovery one day that he was very good at sports.

"Not tennis or golf," he told her, his voice low and quiet-sounding as they sat in the darkened room, she on the couch, he on the floor, and Ajax staring in on them as if she'd been invited. "I didn't like either of those. My father played those games; maybe that was why. I tried football but it seemed kind of—senseless to me. Then, I was looking through some of my mother's things one day, personal things she left me, and I saw my parents together, as teenagers, in Norway. They

came over here when Dad was very young and he and
my uncles got rich very quickly. But in that snapshot,
they were all young and they'd been skiing and they
looked so—right, together. It wasn't until he started
making the money, investing in films and things, that
the trouble started between them."

And that was when he had decided to trying skiing.
Within ten years—he was now twenty-six—he had become world-renowned, a fast, graceful phenomenon
who won every race he entered, who took awards and
gold cups by the dozens, and who became the darling of
the wealthy jet set. He didn't tell Jamie that, but they
both knew it was true.

She had gotten very, very sleepy, and the last question had seemed as if she might have dreamed it, not
really asked it.

"What about Ajax, Thorne? What makes you think
you have to try Silverlode? What makes you so—
certain—"

His voice had come to her from what seemed like
very far away:

". . . last love affair. And the most wonderful, most
exciting trip of all—"

She'd gone to sleep, to wake up in absolute panic.
Late again for work! David would fire her; he'd be furious, after the last time, when she'd promised never,
never again would her work suffer because of Thorne
or anyone else.

"It's terribly, horribly unfair," she'd said as a weary
Thorne drove her down the mountain and into Aspen.
"He pays me all that money and now he's had to get his
own breakfast—"

"Don't tell me you fix his breakfast?" There was a
definite edge to Thorne's voice. "I can't see any reason-
ing in that," he said. "He's got a couple living in with
him, hasn't he? And he didn't hire you as a cook, did
he?"

She knew Thorne was edgy; they'd slept only a couple of hours and he had wanted very badly to make

love, but she'd told him no. Now, he was suddenly showing himself to be jealous of David.

"I do it because I have to get up early anyway, to begin typing. Thorne, can't you go a little faster, please?"

"I'm not going to kill us both because of some boring book he's trying to write."

"It isn't boring! Please—let's not be unkind to each other."

In front of David's house, where lights burned in the study and the kitchen area, he pulled her into his arms.

"I hope that does it," he said.

"What?"

"Talking. The big interrogation. I hope that does it."

She put her hands gently on his face. "Do you know what I think? I honestly think—the more you talk to me, the more I love you."

She had not meant to say that; it had simply come out of her, out of her worried, loving heart. She had not meant to tell him how she felt about him; it was rather humiliating, since he had never told her he loved her.

"Let's have dinner," he told her. "Early."

"I'll have to check with David. After all, he's going to be furious." She looked rather anxiously toward the house.

"Are you sure you want to go on living in his house, Jamie?"

"Please," she said gently, "you mustn't start thinking that way. David and I are good friends and he's always been a perfect gentleman."

"You're sure?"

"Of course I'm sure." She wondered if she should tell him now that he wasn't going to ski down Ajax, that already David had set things in motion to stop the exhibition. She decided against it; she was in no mood for Thorne's explosion, and there would be one, she felt certain.

Jamie got out of the car and, as she'd done before, went into David's house feeling guilty and anxious. She heard some sound coming from the kitchen; he was very likely fixing himself breakfast, dropping pans, cursing, getting angrier by the minute.

She hurried up to her room and quickly took off the clothes she'd worn on her date with Thorne, getting into her usual comfortable jeans and woolly sweater. Then she glanced at herself in the mirror; her hair looked uncombed and her face looked at once sleepy and yet glowing.

I look like a girl who has been made love to, she thought wryly, remembering the long hours of coffee and conversation. Well, perhaps they had become closer last night; she certainly felt closer to him. Maybe what they had done had, in the last analysis, been more loving than physical sex.

Jamie let her mind flee back to a moment, remembering how, around two in the morning, they'd fried eggs and had eaten them, sometimes smiling at each other across the small Danish table in the kitchen. Yes, they'd been very close.

She decided not to bother combing her hair; she'd do it later. Every second she spent here in her bedroom probably meant David's wrath had risen ten percent. She hurried down the stairs, down the half-flight leading to the underground kitchen, and shoved open the pretty Dutch door that led to the main cooking area.

There, she stopped cold.

Rhonda Miles, wearing what was unmistakably David's bathrobe, was pouring coffee from a fragrant-smelling silver pot. There was an air of warmth about the two of them; it was almost as if Jamie had walked into the cozy kitchen of a happily married couple of some years' standing.

David looked stunned, Rhonda, a bit smug.

"Oh," was the first thing Jamie said; she felt horribly embarrassed. "Well, I'll go on up to the study," she said somewhat feebly. "I'll explain—why I'm a little late for work, but not until I've finished with the work on my desk, please."

"No need explaining," David said, his face turning red; "I'll be along in a few minutes. Oh—want coffee?"

"No, thank you." She was glad to be, as it were, excused from that room. Rhonda seemed to have enjoyed every second of it, however; that beautiful redhead had smiled ever so sweetly at Jamie as she passed the sugar bowl to David, her hand graceful and pretty, flashing a very large emerald ring.

"The Danish will be done in a moment," Rhonda said, "darling."

By the time David finally joined Jamie in his study, to begin the day's delayed work, she had brushed her short hair into a dark cap of curls, and she sat at her desk near the window, typing.

David gravely handed her a steaming cup of coffee.

"Do you want to ask me what the devil that wild, spoiled infant of a woman was doing, spending the night in my house?" His brown eyes were unreadable behind his glasses. "Or should I ask you why you decided not to come home last night?"

"David, I only work for you. This is not my home. You've no—"

"By all the gods and little devils," David said suddenly," I believe she set it up! I honestly believed Rhonda wanted you to walk in here and think—" He shook his head, smiling in spite of himself. "I'll never quite be able to figure that one out."

"I think she has you figured out," Jamie told him. "Anyway, I'm awfully glad you two—"

"Rhonda and I are not going through some moronic throes of love, Jamie, so get that notion out of your overly romantic little head." He frowned. "And in spite of what you say, I still feel a responsibility for you. I'm standing here waiting for you to tell me you weren't with Thorne Gundersen all night. Were you?"

"I don't see why you—"

"Because Rhonda told me she'd seen you going up the mountain with Thorne and some friends and you probably would be staying in someplace. Of course, that vicious little witch lied about the whole business, simply because she saw her chance to stay the night here. The Lord knows," he said, "why she'd go to all that trouble just to sleep on my couch!" He glared at Jamie. "And the couch it was. Not that I wasn't tempted, but it isn't sex that one needs, nor money, nor—"

"She loves you, David. I'm sure you know that." Jamie began straightening sheets of paper. "And that is why she wanted to stay here and that is why she fibbed about my not coming home. It just so happens that I didn't, but she didn't know that. She's jealous of me, you see. I'm sure of that." Somehow, what was happening between Rhonda and David seemed very clear to her. She felt certain that they loved each other, but David hadn't discovered that fact yet.

Her own problems with Thorne were not so clear to her.

David held a press conference that afternoon, arranged by his agent, a man who impressed Jamie with his orderliness. The private plane landed exactly when he'd said it would, and by five, David sat in his living room along with Jamie, as he talked to reporters.

He talked about his as yet unfinished book, about "life-styles" and finally about his coming lecture against what he called, "old-fashioned, bloodthirsty ways to produce pleasure, such as watching a man break his back, legs and neck trying to ski down Silverlode."

Listening to him, Jamie felt her insides go cold at the thought of Thorne's body lying twisted and dead under some tree on that dangerous run. But that, she assured herself, would never happen. David was seeing to that.

In fact, he seemed so confident that the exhibition featuring Thorne Gundersen would be canceled, in the interest of safety and sanity, that shortly before they stopped work for the day, he announnced that he'd promised Rhonda he'd go with her party to Las Vegas.

"That means," he said, "that you go along, too, of course. If you've come to think that Aspen is a merry-go-round of parties, sex, booze and drugs, Jamie—wait until you get a load of Vegas!"

CHAPTER IX

"You've a call from the Lodge switchboard," Emma told her that evening. "Urgent, they said."

Urgent. She'd been sitting quietly in her bedroom, writing letters home, waiting with some kind of unreasonable excitement for Thorne's call. David was out for the evening; he hadn't said so, but Jamie felt certain he was with Rhonda.

Her hand trembled on the phone.

"Yes?"

"I have to see you," Thorne told her, his voice strained. "Look—it's terribly important. There's been a lot of scuttle on the runs today about the exhibition."

She should have expected that. "Yes," she said quietly, "I should imagine there would be."

There was a little pause. "Last night—when we were together last night—did you know what Saunders is going to try to do?"

He was angry, furious; she could tell that. Jamie realized she might very well be seeing a totally new side of Thorne—coldly angry, determined that nobody should try to interfere with his plans.

"Yes," she said quietly, "I knew. I should have told you, but—"

"All that time you were asking me about how it was to be a kid growing up in places all over—all the time I was talking to you, telling you things I never tell women—you knew Saunders was planninng to try to stop my run down Silverlode?"

"Thorne—"

"Look," he told her, "I don't really think you understand what I'm talking about."

"Of course I understand. And furthermore—I approve."

"It's terribly important that I see you," he told her, a definite edge to his voice. "I'll be by to pick you up; I'm at the Lodge."

"No," she said quickly. "I'll—get a cab. I'll meet you in the main lounge."

Jamie hung up. The truth was she needed time to gather her thoughts before seeing Thorne, now that he knew of David's campaign to ban the exhibition. Perhaps she should have talked about that the night before; Thorne was probably right about that.

She put on warm boots, a scarf and wool gloves and a heavy, good-looking green tweed coat she'd bought with her first paycheck from David. She was a small girl, short, so sometimes clothes were a problem. But the coat had been perfect, shockingly expensive and in the window of a very exclusive shop in downtown Aspen. Now she had the feeling that whenever she looked at it in the future, she'd remember she'd worn it with Thorne.

Outside, it was early dark; lights were on in all the big houses along the tree-lined streets. Jamie crossed the street, hands in her warm coat pockets. She'd get a cab as she'd said, but for a while she wanted to walk.

She nearly always felt the urge to get up and go from wherever she happened to be at the time, and walk into the mountains, into the snow and greenness of them, where there were no people, no parties, no fast cars, no pull between what she felt for Thorne and what David had hinted to her might be wrong with him. She'd avoided talking to David about Thorne, not only because it had seemed totally disloyal but because she felt David might have something to tell her she didn't want to hear.

And for some strange reason she thought again of the broken glass in Thorne's house. She saw it in her mind as clearly as if it had been put there for a reason. Then, the light changed and she went across the street, walking quickly past the shops where Indian jewelry, chic clothes, hanging plants and hand-carved furniture were displayed. He isn't like Kurt, she thought, forcing herself to look at Ajax, there in the distance. Kurt wanted to ski Silverlode because it would open doors to international invitations to ski in other exhibitions, but Thorne only wants to make it down Silverlode—as if that were some kind of end for him.

The thought came to her as suddenly as the mental picture of the broken glass did: *Thorne knows he won't make it down that run!*

It was such a terrible, earthshaking thought that she had to stop walking for a moment. She found herself near the little corner coffeehouse where her friend Donna worked, and in spite of the fact that Thorne was up there at the Lodge right now, waiting for her, ready to demand things of her she would not do—like get David to stop the ban—she stepped inside the coffeehouse.

It was crowded with the younger crowd, mostly high-school people, children of the very rich who were, for the most part, good-looking and terribly confident of what they had been taught by their parents, namely that a fortune in money meant they need not feel any responsibility for anything or anyone. For the most part, they skied, gave and went to parties, drank too much and were sexually very promiscuous, just like their parents.

Some of them were fifteen or sixteen, but some of the girls were even younger.

"Jamie!" It was Donna, plump, obviously pleased to see Jamie, carrying a tray high above her head. "Hey— find a seat; I'll be over in a minute!"

Jamie stood by the door until Donna hurried over to her.

"I can't stay, Donna. I just wanted to tell you I'm sorry I may have seemed to—"

"I knew you hadn't turned into a social snob, if that's what you mean. I knew you'd get around to coming in to see me." She smiled happily at Jamie. "Guess what? I'm getting married!"

Jamie reached for her friend's hand. "I'm glad—I want to hear all about it." She looked uncertainly toward the Lodge. "I have to meet Thorne in a few minutes. I should be there now."

"Aren't we lucky, Jamie, you and I? Both of us in love— Has he proposed yet, honey?"

"No, not yet." She gave her friend a quick hug. "I'll call you, I promise."

"Send me a card from Vegas; I hear you've been invited aboard Rhonda's private jet. What a life you've found for yourself!"

Yes, what a lonely, mixed-up, unhappy kind of life!

She took a cab the rest of the way. Cars were parked in front of and all around the Lodge; people were being picked up, sometimes by chauffeurs, more often by parents or friends. Thorne's car was there in the parking lot, with fresh snow on its roof. He must have been out on the ski runs all day, Jamie thought, as she pushed open the front doors of the place.

There was, as there always was in this big place, a general feeling of casual affluence; young, good-looking people wearing imported ski sweaters and jeans from Paris or one of the local shops sat around sipping drinks and talking. Jamie had met a lot of them at parties with Thorne, but now, knowing how he would surely hate her before this meeting was over, all the tanned, beautiful faces of the Beautiful People seemed to blur together. People came up and hugged her, some even kissed her lightly as she made her way toward the bar, where Thorne sat with his broad back to her, a glass of brandy between his hands.

"You're going on the jet to Vegas, aren't you, darling? Wonderful!"

"Is it true you've been offered ten thousand dollars to

write your own book about what it's really like under David Saunders' roof?"

"Thorne's looking thoroughly miserable over there, won't talk to a soul. What kind of game are you playing, anyway?"

"She wants him to marry her, idiot."

"Oh, so that's what it's all about."

She pushed her way through, finally standing behind him, feeling a bit breathless.

"Hello."

He swung himself around on the high stool. "I've been sitting here feeling terrible because you took a cab." He stood beside her, taking her arm; in some mysterious way he was always able to take her immediately away from the crowd. First, it was a catching of her mind, a quick union that occurred whenever they were together. Then, his hand would be on hers, or around her waist or resting lightly on her shoulders, and he would take her out of the room. It had happened before, at parties, when the noise was too much, the people too drunk, the smoke too heavy.

Now, they were outside the Lodge, facing the ski runs on the fair side of the mountain, the easier ones.

"Where do you want to go, Jamie? You were right all along, you know. We do have to talk."

She nodded. Inside the Lodge, inside the big glass walls, one could see all the moving, smiling, talking people.

"Not inside anyplace," she said. "Here, I guess. This is okay."

So they sat on one of the benches near the little short run called "Babies,' " and their breath frosted as they spoke.

"It only needs explaining," he told her. They sat facing the moon, not sitting close together. It was as if they both knew this was the leaving, the parting. *It's the end of us*, Jamie thought, and suddenly she didn't want to sit here, friendly and polite; she wanted to go someplace and cry.

"There isn't anything that needs explaining," she said, her voice low but steady. "David is going to stop the Silverlode run. He's already begun doing it."

Thorne was silent for a moment. The moon, a high sliver of a winter moon, watched; it seemed to Jamie that there was no sound in the world just then.

"What about you, Jamie? Are you—helping him do this?"

"Yes," she said quietly, "I am."

"Even though you know what it means to me to go down Ajax? Even though I want that more than anything in the world?"

Now, she thought, *speak the truth to him; if he remembers you in any way at all, let it be honestly!*

"I don't think you really want to do it, Thorne," she said. "I don't understand it—I don't know why it is—but for some reason, you think you have to do that." She took a small breath. "Even though you know as well as I do that you'll never make it."

She thought that would finish it, that he'd get up and walk away from her and it would be finished. But he didn't. Surprisingly, he reached for her hand and held it very tightly.

"This will be the last time," he told her. "I'll make it down and I swear to you—I'll never try another mountain. But you can talk to David, make him lay off. You can do it, Jamie. And I swear," he said, his voice thick with feeling, "I swear I'll never give you cause to worry about me again."

"That," she told him, "is the nearest thing you've ever said about a future for us. I've never been really sure there would be." She held his hand to her face. "I don't want anything to happen to you—that's why, that's what this is all about." She turned to put her lips to his hand, and it was then that she saw the bruise. Very slowly she raised her eyes to meet his.

"You've been hurt. Thorne, would you mind telling me what's going on? Are you in—in some kind of trouble or something?"

"The only trouble I'm in is the trouble your boss is about to give me. You've got to talk him out of this, honey. He's on some kind of—humanity binge, and I'm the first scapegoat!"

"Have you been fighting? Is that how the glass got broken and your hand—"

"I told you about the glass. I bumped into it and it broke, that's all. And last night, I bumped into a lamp. That house I rented has too much stuff in it—a guy can't find his way around in the dark. Jamie, I've been thinking about going with you, to talk to him. There's one thing he's got going for him; he's a gentleman. I'll put it to him that way. But I need you to go with me. Come on," he said, pulling her to her feet, "my car's just outside, in the lot."

"I'm afraid I can't do that," she said. A cold wind had blown in from around the mountains; she began feeling its chill. "It won't help, Thorne. He's going to stop you. And I want him to."

"Now you listen," he said quietly. "If you care about me, you've got to see my side of it. You've got to stop thinking like—like some kind of doting auntie whose afraid I'll break my arm. Speed is my business, Jamie, and you and your boss aren't going to change that. Do you think you can stop people from going down ski slopes or driving race cars or doing anything else they want to do, even though it's dangerous? Tell your bleeding-heart boss it isn't going to work. I'm going down Silverlode just as planned."

There was nothing more to say. She hurried into the Lodge, through the crowds of people. She saw Lydia Murkin at the bar, watching, but nobody tried to stop her. At the door, Thorne came up behind her.

"I'll take you home, Jamie."

She shook her head no, and, fighting tears, hurried down the steps to a waiting taxi.

"I can't take a single, lady," the driver said. "You'll have to wait until I get a carful."

So she sat in the taxi, painfully conscious of Thorne's

presence there on the Lodge porch. He stood, leaning against the log wall, arms folded, watching her, until finally three giggling young girls got into the taxi and the driver started it, heading for town.

David's book was completed the following day; he seemed in very high spirits as he dictated the last page. Jamie tried to share his pride and joy, but inside her there was a heaviness. She'd thought Thorne would call; all day she had thought that, but now, sitting in the quiet of evening, the day's work finished, she had to admit he wasn't going to call. Not ever.

"Call Max in New York and tell him it's done," he told her. "Then, kindly order three dozen roses, white."

"For Rhonda?"

"Of course not for Rhonda. Nobody ever sends Rhonda flowers."

"David, did you hear what you just said?"

He'd been smiling; his face was flushed with triumph and from a glass of brandy he'd raised in a salute to "chapter twenty-seven, where they all get their just dues and live miserably ever after."

"What I just said was that nobody sends Rhonda flowers." He was silent for a second or two. "All right," he said finally, sitting heavily in his chair near the fireplace, "I know, I know. I've treated her badly, I suppose, allowing her to drag me off to those stupid, boring parties, allowing her to fancy that I might—care about her." His eyes held worry. He took off his glasses and cleaned them; Jamie sensed a new sadness in him. "I should never have let her stay here the other night," he said. "She seemed sure you wouldn't be coming in at all, and she looked so—like a kitten or something. Usually, Rhonda is all cat; tigress is a better word, I believe. But—" his voice warmed, "she can be a kitten, too, sometimes, the kind you find in dark doorways, the kind that cries a lot."

"You're in love with her, David."

"Oh, rubbish." He glared at her. "In love? What the

devil is *that* supposed to mean? That I'm in today and out tomorrow, maybe? It doesn't work that way, little girl. And if you don't know that, you're in for a very bad time. I've told you that. Now, before long, you're going to find it out for yourself." He stood up. "Look—I've worked long and hard on this book. Now, it's finished. So let's celebrate and not worry about anything. Hard to do in this life, but every so often, the lucky ones can manage a few hours without feeling the miseries of the world. I'll take you to Zach's, okay? Even you will like the French cooking there."

She gave him a small, grateful smile. He knew her, knew her mind and feelings. He very likely sensed that she had broken up with Thorne. They hadn't spoken of him all day, except that David had mentioned some phone calls from various newspapers around the country, and one straight from The Associated Press. They'd wanted to know about his forthcoming lecture, about why he chose to hold up skiing as a kind of slaughter.

"What those idiots don't understand," he told Jamie as they drove up to Zach's, a delightfully small and very elegant place famous since the claim jumpers and mine shafters got rich there, "is that it isn't the sport I'm knocking—it's the attitude of the people who go to watch it. Don't tell me that crowds who go to see the Grand Prix aren't secretly hoping one of the heroes will end up in pieces somewhere along the way."

Now, sitting in the quiet restaurant, with the mountains rising beyond like steadfast ghosts, and soft candlelight between them, Jamie looked into David's brown eyes and suddenly she wanted all pretense to be gone between them.

"Maybe it's time for me to give the advice, David. If I do—will you please listen?"

He frowned. "I'm saving your blue-eyed boyfriend's skin for him, and that fact alone means you must not give me advice, ever. I consider myself above advice." He finished his wine. "Actually, I brought you here to discuss my newest idea for my next novel."

"That's very nice," she said stubbornly, "but I want to talk about Rhonda. What right do you have to put her down simply because she's rich and beautiful?"

"Will you kindly stop dragging her into our conversation?" His voice had risen; he looked around him, lowered his tone and held onto her hands almost, she thought, with desperation. "My idea is about an older, worldly man who is very lonely after the death of his wife. Then, one day, a kind of—of princess comes to his door and asks to be let in. Now this man has always been an exceedingly great fool, but this time he is given the wisdom to open the door and let this lovely creature into his house. There, she gave him peace and his sense of humor began to come back to him, so that he could do his work once again." He touched her cheek. "So, in order not to lose this friend, he asks her to marry him."

She felt the breath stop in her for an instant. Marry David? There he was, not old at all, not creaky at all, but instead, a man who was perhaps at his peak. Plus, he had the wisdom about life that Thorne did not have and possibly could not have because he was too young still.

"I'm very honored," she said finally, her voice gentle. "But it's no good marrying people when you happen to be in love with other people."

"There's that idiotic combination of words again." He let go of her hands and began fumbling at his clothes for his pipe. "I'm offering you friendship, a good life of traveling and reading, a house wherever you happen to want it—and you're prattling about some state of mind that, I understand, transports one into the same frame of mind that schizophrenics have." His eyes were stern as he began puffing away on his pipe. It was hard, in that moment, to believe that he had just proposed marriage to her. "You don't know a damned thing about loving, Jamie. I suppose that comes as a very great shock to you. It usually does, to girls who think they'd go to the moon or anywhere else because they're in some state of mental retardation."

She was beyond getting furious with him. "That's not," she told him, "a very nice thing to say to someone you just proposed to."

"Let me tell you about loving, Jamie." He leaned back in his chair for a moment. Outside, the moonlight lay spilled across the frozen snow, so beautiful that for a second she thought of him, of Thorne. There was an unfinished feeling inside her, more than just the anguish of a lost love. She'd never felt this way before about a man, never. And yet David kept telling her she knew nothing at all about loving.

"All right," she said, "since I'm a complete shell, someone who doesn't know about loving, kindly give me a lesson. But why you'd even consider marrying me—"

"Because you're like a child," he told her, his voice suddenly kind. "In many ways, you're like Margo. You've never seen a picture of her, have you?" He reached into his wallet. For a moment she tried to take him seriously; he actually *had* asked her to be his wife. Now that she knew he thought of her as a friend, nothing at the moment, seemed more appealing than the thought of spending her life with someone who did not make her angry, or hurt her. Marriage with a friend, she thought. And then Rhonda's lovely face came into her mind, the silver-gray eyes, the exquisite clothes, the air of absolute sophistication and coolness.

David had said that sometimes Rhonda was like a small, helpless and lost kitten. The kind that cries.

She could not do it. She could never marry him, not when another woman loved and needed him so much. Even though he didn't seem at all inclined to propose that he and Rhonda do much more than spend time together at a party—she could not do it.

He was holding out a picture of his wife, Margo.

"We took it at Tahoe," he said. "She used to love it there. We had a home there; I bought it for her right after my agent sold the movie rights to *All That Glitters*. I sold it after she died, and all her furniture. I suppose I knew that, if I kept it all, I'd end up one of those crazies who walks around in the past, not changing one piece of anything." He looked at her. "Do you think I'm one of those crazies, Jamie? Do you by any chance think that the reason I'm proposing to you is because I'm afraid to spend my life with the woman who wants me to do that very much?"

"Yes," she said quietly, "I think you've asked me to marry you because you're still in hiding. But it was a very sweet idea, all the same."

David sighed and raised his glass to her. "Here," he said, "is to what was a very sweet, but probably stupid, idea."

Jamie found herself concentrating on the small picture, a tiny color portrait, that of a woman sitting by a window with her hands crossed in her lap. She wore a soft looking dress and the light softly touched her face and hair.

She was not beautiful. She was, Jamie saw with a mental start, not even plain; she was, in terms of classical, accepted beauty-forms, homely. She leaned closer to look. What had there been about this slender, rather fragile-looking woman with her long dark hair and her unlovely face? Jamie saw it then, some fleeting look of magic there was about the small smile, the merry eyes.

"She was a blithe spirit," David said softly.

So that had been her secret, her secret of holding a man in her arms even after her death. *Poor Rhonda*, Jamie thought.

At the end of the meal, just before a flaming tray of sweets was brought in, Jamie looked again at David and smiled.

"Are you ready for my advice now?"

"I'll never be ready for advice from babies."

"You mean because you've had a great love in your life and so far all I've been able to do is feel something close to hero worship for Thorne?"

"Something like that," he said rather grumpily. He

looked at his watch. "It's still early—we could go some-place else."

"David, you know perfectly well you're bored with nightlife. Let's go home and I'll make you a very good cup of coffee." She realized how very dear this man was to her. "My advice," she said, as he helped her into her wool coat, "is to think about life without being loved. I imagine it's very lonely. Perhaps you don't know how lucky you are, being loved by Rhonda."

"Most of the time she's impossibly spoiled, nasty, witchy and—"

"But not," Jamie said sweetly, "all the time. Ready to go, David?"

For some unaccountable reason, she dreamed of birds that night, white and beautiful, soaring over mountains. She, in her dream, stood somewhere at the bottom of a great mountain, watching. But those were birds; Thorne was a man, made of flesh and blood that would splinter and gush when he fell, going down that run at an incredibly fast speed—

She woke up with a jerk. It was late, later than usual, nearly eight-thirty, but David had told her she was on vacation, now that the novel was finished. Vacation with pay, he'd told her. How very nice, she thought as she got out of bed. There would have been free hours to spend with Thorne, to go to the slopes with him, to watch him practice. Perhaps she could have gone to his house to cook for him.

Except that he hadn't called and wasn't likely to. She knew what it was he wanted: he wanted her to convince David to stop trying to "meddle" in the exhibition. He wanted her to get David to "lay off."

There was a knock at the door and Emma came in, carrying a tray.

"You shouldn't have done that," Jamie told her. "I'm used to getting my own breakfast, you know. But it was very sweet of you."

Usually, when Emma brought the trays in at teatime, into David's study, she put the evening papers on the tray, but this morning, there were none.

"If you're wonderin' about the papers," Emma said, pulling the blinds up, letting in the bright sunshine, "he's got them downstairs." Her eyes looked evasively the other way. "Mr. Saunders wants you to join him downstairs after you've braced yourself with coffee."

"Braced myself? Emma—what's happened?" Fear, cold and quick as a sharp steel knife, touched her heart. "Has there been an accident?" she asked quietly.

"Oh, no—nothin' like that. You'd better go and talk to him. But no sense in gettin' all riled up." But at the door, she turned with sorrowful eyes. "It's my fault," she said, and quite suddenly she burst into tears. "I should never have—said to her what I did. I thought—I thought you were a different type, but you aren't. I never should have talked to that newspaperwoman!"

"Emma—you mean you told Lydia Markin about that night you saw me on the stairs with David? But that wasn't—that was perfectly innocent!"

The woman nodded miserably. "I know that," she said, "now, I know that. But I was afraid you'd come between him and Miss Miles—she loves him and needs him, only he don't know that." She shook her head. "Now, I've caused all kinds of trouble for you and him—and Rhonda Miles is going to get the wrong idea and be unhappy—" She blew her nose. "I ought to be punished for my tongue," she said.

Jamie skipped her usual morning shower so that she could get downstairs as quickly as possible. She had planned to spend the day with her friend Donna; now she was faced with the prospect of some kind of trouble before breakfast.

David was in the living room; the floor was covered with scattered newspapers.

"I can't believe how many papers carry that viper's column," he said, as soon as Jamie came into the room.

"What's been said about us?" She walked closer to

him, remembering the vicious face of the newspaper-woman when she'd watched Jamie leave the Lodge with Thorne, when she'd watched them at parties together, when she'd told Jamie she hadn't been able to "figure out whose girl you are."

He tossed a paper at her. "Nothing, except that she's made it sound like the usual. And there is nothing at all usual about you."

The paper was wrinkled beyond repair; Jamie struggled to get it straight. "David, you aren't being very clear, you know. I can't even find—" She saw it then. "Tattle-tales," was the name of the column, and in it various hints were made as to the identity of people who were doing various forbidden things, but toward the bottom of the gossip, names were suddenly used, real names.

"Thorne Gundersen, that beautiful dreamer who believes he can successfully ski down Silverlode Run next week, has done it again—broken a heart, that is. He was seen dumping his current girlfriend, who went running right back into the arms of her bossy, but benevolent employer, with whom she lives, by the way. Could it *be that this very sassy lady is traveling to Vegas with her oh-so-rich boss before very long, and that ex-lover T. G. is going to be on board the private jet, too? Ho hum—he'd tired of her anyway—*"

She felt the blood leave her face. Then, in a sudden rush of anger, Jamie poured herself a cup of coffee from David's breakfast tray.

"No one listens to her." Her small hand trembled on the cup. "Do they? David—do they? I mean, everyone knows it's all rubbish and—and dirty lies—don't they?"

He shrugged. "The thing is, my little buddy, this happens all the time around here. People shift sex partners like they'd change clothes; it doesn't have any meaning for them, most of the time, because they're zombies, zombies going through some kind of ritual, eating the best food, wearing the most expensive clothes, driving the best cars—and they're zombies." He came over and put his hands on her shoulders. "But you, Jamie dear, are not. And that is why it makes me so dammed mad to make it sound usual, because you're a very unusual girl. I may have to throttle that broad," he said darkly.

She drank her coffee, looking out at the mountains. Thorne was probably out there today, on the far side of Ajax, practicing.

And he had very likely seen the morning papers.

CHAPTER X

The coffeehouse was crowded; it was nearly noon. Jamie had decided to visit Donna after she'd reread that nasty item in the paper once again. Finally, because David had said it was futile to complain or try to do anything about it, she'd put on her coat and left David's house to walk the few blocks to town and the little place where Donna worked.

For a change, her friend didn't look as if she was about to break into a hearty laugh. In fact, when she plopped beside Jamie in the back booth, her round face looked plainly worried.

"I read the paper this morning. I was hoping you'd come in; if you hadn't, I was going over to Saunders' house and talk to you." She pressed Jamie's hand. "I know it's all a lie. You ought to sue."

"I'm all right," Jamie said. "Donna—tell me about your man, about your wedding."

They talked for the better part of an hour, the two of them, heads close together, there in the noisy, busy café. Donna was quitting her job, she said, at the end of the day; she'd stay an extra hour to make up for this "gab session" with Jamie.

"I'm sorry it didn't work out for you and Thorne," Donna said finally. "I just never believed he was using you. That's why I'm glad I'm marrying a nice, simple busboy from the Lodge, who'll take me back to New Jersey and a big Irish family."

Jamie suddenly felt a vast sense of unhappiness wash over her. She had very definitely made up her mind not to be hurt because Thorne was obviously through with her. After all, she had walked out on him, too, if one wanted to come down to the common, nasty level of which lover left first. She pushed the feeling away.

She had told herself the agony of losing him through death would be so terrible that this little pain of simply losing him because she didn't want him to risk dying—that she could take.

And she was taking it. She was doing fine, even looking forward to the trip to Las Vegas. Thorne was going to live, for the time being at least, until he found some other crazy way to destroy himself. In the meantime, there was always the possibility that someday he might seek her out and want to begin again.

Or was that just more of her romantic wishful thinking, as David liked to call it?

"Thorne didn't use me in the way you're thinking," Jamie told her friend. "It wasn't like that, not at all." She smiled. "I'm very glad I met him."

"Have you watched him practice on the runs lately?"

"No." It had troubled her, that he did not seem too interested in practicing daily.

"They're saying he's in very bad form. That he drinks too much and behaves as if he's lost his mind."

Once again, Jamie had that feeling of worry come to her. Yes, yes, he had been behaving oddly. It was true that he partied far too much for a man who ought to stay in tip-top shape, no matter what, since every nerve in his body was going to be tested if he went down that mountain as fast as a train. *It's going to be okay,* she told herself. *David won't let that happen!*

But when Jamie got back to the house, she found out that even David—with all his good intentions and the relative power and influence he had—might not be able to do one single thing to ban that exhibition.

There were reporters there from various papers; apparently his agent had called a press conference. David, charming and relaxed, introduced Jamie to them all.

But when they'd left, when he finally sank into his favorite chair and raised his head to look directly at her, she saw that he was very tired and his eyes held a bitter look.

"I'm not sure it's going to work, Jamie."

She was emptying ashtrays—the reporters had all smoked like stevedores. Suddenly she realized what he was telling her. He didn't mean his book; it had nothing to do with his book.

"David—you said—you said you could stop it! You said you were sure—"

"I didn't say I was sure!" He got up and went to the window. It was turning very cold outside, with new snow expected that evening. In Aspen, people were saying the weather conditions would be perfect for the try down Silverlode. "How could I promise you a thing like that?"

"But you—seemed so confident—" Horror was washing over her. What if he couldn't stop Thorne? What if—

"I was confident, a lot more confident than I am right now." He turned to look at her. "Maybe I live in a dream world. Anyway, my erstwhile buddies from the papers seem to think there's not the remotest chance that this carnival is going to close down simply because a man's life is at stake!" He shook his head. "But I'm not giving up. First, I'll talk about nothing else on the Vegas trip; I'll get everybody all geared up, get them on a new high. They love causes—most of 'em spend half their lives collecting money to give to charity, when they haven't the least idea of what the word really means."

I can't carry this burden, Jamie thought, and she suddenly realized something she hadn't known for sure before. She loved Thorne; not in the groupie, hero-worshiping, childish way David seemed to think she did, but in a profoundly troubling way that was making her choose between her own life and Thorne's.

She chose her own. She chose not to let his death

destroy her, because, like herself, he had a choice to make.

But why is he choosing to wipe himself out?

She went over and gently kissed David's cheek. "I know you're going to try. Good night, David."

His voice stopped her at the door. "Jamie? If I can't stop him, and if he doesn't make it—what then? Are you going to fall apart and quit working for me and all the rest of it?"

"I'm not going to stay around to watch him, if that's what you mean."

She took a long bath and got into her robe. She'd pack for the Las Vegas jaunt in the morning; Rhonda had called and left a message that she was having all her guests picked up early in the morning. But shortly before seven, as Jamie was seriously considering taking a long walk, even if the snow was coming down heavily, she saw Rhonda's green Porsche pull up in front of the house. *Good*, she thought. *I've given David all the help and comfort I can; now he needs more than just friendship and goodwill. He needs a woman to love him.*

They were putting lights up and down other mountains, probably so people could stand there and watch Thorne practice. She sat on her bed, looking at the strings of glittering amber that lined the mountainside. *I can't help you now, my love. Only God can help you now. I can't get you down that run safely.*

She slept, dreaming, as the amber lights from the mountain shone upon her face, of shattered pieces of glass.

It was a remarkably well-equipped jet; not as large as a commercial plane, of course, but so plush inside that David began making bad jokes about it at once. He found a seat for Jamie, settled himself next to her and proceeded to tell his jokes.

Jamie listened with only half an ear; she was watching for the arrival of Rhonda. She wished she dare ask

David where he and Rhonda had gone the night before, and what they had talked about—after all, the two of them were friends and she wanted him to be happy as much as she wanted Thorne to live. Because in a sense she loved them both.

Suddenly, the now-familiar green Porsche appeared on the runway, going at a breakneck speed. It was Rhonda, of course, zooming for dear life out toward the jet and her merry guests.

"What an entrance," David said dryly from beside her. "And she's got company, if you haven't noticed."

She hadn't, but now Jamie leaned closer to the window to look. Her heart seemed to stop, then began pounding in a mixture of joy and deep worry.

It was Thorne, sitting beside Rhonda, both of them having a high old time, nearly late for the party she was giving. Rhonda got out of the car, tossing her gorgeous coppery hair over her shoulders, and then she put her arm around Thorne, so that they appeared to be hugging. And there beside her, David suddenly got very angry.

"Damn him—he's had a go at you and now he's after Rhonda. I ought to get off this plane and punch his face."

"It's all right," Jamie said quietly. "Stop getting so excited and stop being so jealous."

"I am not jealous." He looked at her. "And why aren't you reeling with jealously yourself? After all, you're still in love with that ape, aren't you?"

She ignored his question, watching as Rhonda, her arm still around Thorne, came up the steps to the plane. Thorne stumbled once and nearly fell, then he began laughing as if he knew some secret joke. He'd obviously been drinking but he was far from drunk.

"It's all an act," Jamie said suddenly. She looked at David, who was busily pretending not to care by way of reading a magazine. "David—she keeps glancing up here at the plane to see if you're looking."

"Well, I'm not," he said, turning the page.

Rhonda was now hugging everybody, laughing a lot and looking around for champagne. There at the plane's entrance, near the bar, Thorne looked over Rhonda's head, directly at Jamie.

It was a second of absolute silence for her; it was as if all the sounds in that plane were shut off, even the revving of the speaker system; somebody had been saying five minutes before takeoff.

The world became, in that instant, a place of joy again for her. When he looked into her eyes from perhaps ten feet away, over the heads of the others, there were only the two of them. She held her breath; it was as if he were speaking to her silently, desperately.

"Would you like a drink?" It was David's voice. "Frankly, that weird display of instant love was a bit too much for me."

The moment was gone, lost in the sudden surge of voices, people milling around carrying glasses, a pretty stewardess serving trays of sandwiches and coffee.

"Just coffee, thanks." She wondered if that was the absolute end of them, of Thorne and herself, or if there might be another moment. No matter what, he had no business being on this plane.

David said as much when he came back with a drink for himself and coffee in a paper cup for Jamie. He sat down and, ignoring the Fasten Seat Belts sign, proceeded to talk to her in a low, earnest voice. Under other circumstances, it would have been amusing to watch this poor man, this man who loved Rhonda but perhaps didn't know it, this good, wise man who had been like a loving brother to Jamie.

"It could be insanity," he said. "Just because he skis, it doesn't mean he's got all his bolts in right."

"He's sane, David. And you're still being jealous, which is foolish."

"I've no reason to be jealous," he said somewhat smugly. "As a matter of fact, the lady proposed to me last night, in her car."

So that's what had been going on between the two of them—Rhonda had asked David to marry her!

"You ought to be very complimented and grateful," she told him. "Instead here you are, looking fierce and grumpy and very—nasty." She whispered the last word, because Rhonda was coming toward them, smiling. She looked perfect; her hair was lovely and sleekly clean, her clothes just right for the elegant-yet-humble theme of the trip, which simply meant the people going on the plane wore jeans and jean jackets, most of them, and expensive, hand-tooled boots. But on board the plane, beer and coffee and even mixed drinks came in plain paper cups, and the sandwiches were thick, "cowboy" style, and the hostess on board, hired for the flight there and back, had been asked to wear Western clothes, which included tight jeans and a cowgirl hat pushed off her pretty forehead.

"Having fun, darlings?" Rhonda leaned over them, smiling. "We're getting a game of blackjack going. Why don't you join us?"

"I never gamble," David said, finishing his drink.

Rhonda smiled woodenly. "We all know that, darling. See you later."

They all had to go to their seats as the plane taxied and got into position for takeoff. But as soon as they were airborne, all the guests, or at least most of them, were either gathered around the bar or else already losing large sums of money by gambling in the rear of the plane.

"Lord," David said wearily, closing his eyes, "they can't even wait to make fools of themselves until we land. Tell me when Sally Von Lieber takes off her bra and tries to take bets on the size. She does that all the time, and that," he said, "is when I want to get off this airplane."

Thorne was back there with them, apparently gambling quite heavily. A girl, lovely as an exquisite flower, hurried toward the bar to get another drink for Thorne, carefully avoiding looking at Jamie as she sped back to the gamblers. *What's wrong?* Jamie thought, closing her eyes, her head back on the seat. Beside her, David had fallen silent, too.

"David?"

"We just crossed over into Nevada. I've flown this route so many times I can tell when we're getting close to Vegas. It has a certain smell about it that's unmistakable."

"Did you say—did I hear you say the other morning that your doctor friend, Mel, is taking a weekend off to go to Vegas?"

"The ambition of Mel's life, besides to save lives like a good doctor should, is to have a date with Angel O'Hara. And she's in Vegas at the moment, at the Copa, I think. At any rate, so is good old Doc."

"Twenty-one!" a woman screeched from the back of the plane, and as she did, the thousands and thousands of lights from Vegas began to appear, like upside-down stars.

"Will you be seeing him?"

"If I want to hang out at the Copa Lounge all of the time, yes. But I don't plan to do that." He looked at her. "Why all the questions about Mel?"

"I want to talk to him, that's all. Will you ask him to call me at our hotel?"

"Sure." He hooked her safety belt for her; in seconds the lights had become distinct and glittering. "Don't say 'our' hotel that way. Rhonda is furious because of that blurb in the papers. And even madder when she asked me to marry her and I told her no."

"No isn't forever," Jamie said, reaching over to fasten his seat belt for him.

The call to take seats came from the pilot; Thorne sat across from her, next to the pretty young girl who talked in a loud, overly excited voice, thinking she was special because he'd chosen to sit next to her.

As the plane's wheels touched smoothly on the landing strip, Jamie turned her head to look at Thorne. She thought he would not acknowledge her boldness, but he did. He turned his head briefly, as the girl beside him pretended to be frightened, and as she hugged him, his blue eyes once again met Jamie's.

The intensity of his look grabbed her heart. She knew something was wrong; she had known that for some time. It was something else, something more, than his just wanting to ski down a mountain. Whatever the driving force was that led him to the edge of death, it had something to do with all the fragments and pieces of things she might very likely have forgotten, except that their relationship had always been somehow off balance, veering too far to the other side of honesty.

Thorne had a secret, and the secret was going to kill him on the mountain Ajax. Jamie meant to find out what that secret was, before it was too late.

She felt David's hand press hers in fellowship as the plane taxied to a stop and people began tumbling out of seats, everybody loud and anxious to start hitting the big gambling casinos.

"I'm going to have a talk with each and every one of them," David told her, "If I can get enough people to sign a petition, we still might be able to stop him."

She nodded, tears behind her eyes. But as she squeezed past Thorne and the girl in the aisle, Jamie managed a bright, fake smile.

"Hope you get in some practice here, Thorne."

"Darlin'," the girl said, hanging onto his arm, "he's had *plenty* of practice!"

"I was talking about skiing," Jamie said, as David led her down the aisle.

There were various station wagons waiting outside, to take them all to the hotel where Rhonda, though miffed at David, had leased rooms for her entire party in honor of David's birthday.

"That's poppycock and rubbish," he said later, in the hotel coffee shop. He'd phoned Jamie in her room and asked her to meet him there, before the "evening's insanity" began. "Rhonda was just looking for an excuse to drag a bunch of people over here and spend her money. Or rather, her grandfather's money."

Jamie had never seen a place like this one. She had never seen such beautiful women; they seemed to be everywhere, walking alone in the plush bars, through the crowds who were absorbed in gambling; even on the streets there were beautiful-looking women alone.

"Ladies of the evening," David told Jamie in a fatherly tone, as a girl walked by and gave him a long, meaningful look. "Every whore, pimp, thief and con artist hits this town at one time or another. We don't have to stick with Rhonda's group, you know. We can go find Mel and watch what's-her-name."

"I'll be ready in fifteen minutes," she told him.

"Make that ten." She got up from the table, picking up her purse.

David watched her. "You certainly are in a hurry for me to find Mel for you." His intelligent eyes narrowed behind his glasses. "Do you by any chance think Thorne is sick?"

"No—not sick. But he might—there might be something—"

"Mental illness? Are you suggesting that?"

She let her breath out. "David—I don't know; I only thought maybe a doctor could tell what's wrong. Because something is."

"Obviously. A man who is about to ski down the most dangerous mountain in the world, on the run so many men have been killed trying, doesn't party days before he's supposed to try to ski." He puffed on his pipe. "I've seen him work, in Switzerland, in the French Alps. He's fast and he takes chances, but he's always been known as a man of great skill and precision. Now, he won't even be able to put on his skis, let alone make it down that damned mountain." His eyes looked into hers. "No matter what—will you be okay?"

Jamie hesitated for a moment. "I thought I would be," she said, her voice soft. "I honestly thought I could

make a choice and decide to live and—and be happy
and forget about Thorne. I mean, if he's stupid enough
to want to die when he doesn't have to, then that's his
choice, isn't it?" She lowered her eyes. "I thought I
could feel that way about him—but the truth is, I
can't." Tears came to her eyes. "I don't want him to
die, David. I—don't think I can go on if he does."

They were very close at that moment, in that busy
coffee shop, where gamblers wandered in to try to wake
up. Outside, neon lights blazed, and in the adjoining
casino, they could hear the loud bark of the stickmen at
tables.

She felt his fingers, very gentle, on her wet cheek.

"I guess," he said quietly, "I was wrong. You do love
him. And that changes you from a little girl with stars in
her eyes to a woman, Jamie."

"Then you'll talk to Mel?"

"We can go find him right now. I'm sure he's sitting
at the Copa staring at what's-her-name."

They left a few moments later, to go to the Copa. On
the way through the hotel lobby, Freddie Collier, heir to
a vast fortune acquired by his grandfather in various
shady deals concerning California land, suddenly came
up from behind and grabbed Jamie's arm. He was a spi-
dery little fellow, the kind of young man one might expect to see working at the docks in Dublin, all freckles
and fair skin. He looked out of place in his expensive
clothes, but actually, he wasn't. Freddie had been born
rich and, having used him as a character long ago in
one of his earlier novels, David had dismissed him as
being "stupid, lazy and extremely boring."

"Rhonda's lining everybody up for dinner. She told
me you two would probably be off hiding someplace."
He smirked. "Now why don't you both be nice and
come to the party?"

Jamie looked hopelessly at David. "We're coming,"
he said smoothly. "Tell Rhonda I've just gone to get
good old Mel, doctor at large. We'll be along for her
dinner, don't worry."

And so, Jamie hoped, would Thorne.

The singer named Angel stood in a pink spotlight which turned her bleached hair pink. She sang in a husky voice, smiling now and again at the enraptured Mel, who grinned like a schoolboy whenever she did.

"Surprise," David said, sitting down at his table. "You remember my secretary, Jamie."

Mel shook her hand. "What brings you guys to Vegas?" He didn't seem very interested; he'd once again turned to face the girl on the stage, just beyond them.

"We've come to take you away from all this," David said.

"Not now, buddy. She's going to sing 'Body and Soul' for her next number."

"Well, you'll just have to catch that later." David leaned closer. "Someone may need you very badly."

"Somebody sick?"

"That's for you to find out. So come on."

Mel sighed. "Okay, but of all the doctors in town, why me?" However, he was already halfway up out of his seat. "Now," he said at the door, "she'll probably never sing at me again like that."

Rhonda's "group" had been seated in the main show lounge, they were told. Dinner had been ordered, but they could order late.

"I thought someone was supposed to need a doctor," Mel said crossly. "Look—I detest large groups eating the crummy food these hotels put out. Why'm I here with you? What's going on?"

"Never mind," David told him. "Just mingle, will you?"

There was plenty of that going on; nobody seemed to stay put at the long table for very long. A comic came out and told some filthy jokes, then a singer and then another comic. Jamie, sitting next to David, picked at her salad and tried not to watch as Thorne, sitting across from her and down, toward Rhonda, ordered another glass of wine. In no time at all, people started moving away from the dining room out to the huge room where the gambling took place. Thorne left with Rhonda and a few others, then David followed, taking a mildly protesting Mel with him. Jamie had promised to come along, but actually she hated the thought of going in there. Watching Thorne behave that way made her feel angry and hopeless, as if she were watching him walk some kind of narrow railing fifty stories up.

"Come on," Freddie said from across the table, "cheer up. Here, come help me lose some money; want to?"

"No, thanks, Freddie—I think I'll just go on up to my room."

"You didn't come to Vegas to sit in your room, honey, did you?"

Why had she come? To please David, maybe. Perhaps because she was uneasy, staying in Aspen alone, without David's company and the household she'd quickly gotten to enjoy. Or perhaps she had come to run away from Thorne, from the pain of his rejection—

"Come on," Freddie was saying, "let's go play some twenty-one."

She looked at this little man. He'd changed his clothes from what he'd worn on the plane; now he wore slacks and a blazer jacket and a silk scarf tied at the throat. He looked a little drunk as he stood there, weaving and grinning. "Come on," he said again, reaching for her playfully, pulling her close to him. "If you'd honestly rather go to your room, how about a little company?"

She pulled away, but before she could step away from him completely and get on the elevator. Thorne came runing across the room. That's what he was doing, running, as if to save her from drowning, or from being run over by a train. He lowered his head like a bull or a football player and simply charged directly into poor Freddie.

There were curses, shouts, men running over to help

or hinder, and then Freddie was standing there with a bleeding nose, saying he was going to sue. Someone snapped a picture, and at that point Thorne grabbed Jamie, pushed his way through the crowd with her hand in his, and then they were out on the busy street, hurrying along the sidewalk, past the spraying fountains of multicolored water and the big hotels and the well-dressed people getting in and out of cars in front of the hotels.

They walked a long time, very fast; Jamie had to hurry to keep up with him. Finally, she stopped, panting a little, and tugged at his sleeve.

"Thorne—what's this all about?" But she was, she realized, happy to be with him, glad to be near him, walking, running, whatever. "Freddie didn't—he didn't mean—"

"Of course he meant to. And I couldn't stand it." He looked at her, his eyes going quickly over her face, as if he were looking for something. "You don't really want to go back there, do you?"

"No," she said, and she took his arm.

They walked for blocks; the night air was sharp and cold. Beyond the gaudy, blazing lights that went on and off like mad, winking eyes lay the desert, serene, silent, and, Jamie thought, very beautiful.

"Are you tired yet?"

"Should I be tired?"

He stopped walking. "I wanted you to be tired so I could carry you." A taxi honked at them and he grabbed her hand and hurried her across the street. "I want to spend the night with you, Jamie."

Her heart began pounding in her ears; one moment not so many moments ago, she had been on her way to her room and now, suddenly, she was having all those wild feelings again. Hold me, she thought, hold me—

"Will you?"

For a night. That was what he was talking about, for one night.

"I make it a practice never to go to bed with strangers."

The lovely glow of those past few moments, when they'd walked along, was gone. Now, suddenly, they were on the verge of anger.

"I'm supposed to react to that, right? I'm supposed to get mad at you and let you walk away from me, back to the hotel." He put his hands on her shoulders as people pushed by them; the sidewalks were jammed with laughing, talking, pushing people.

"Thorne, it's very flattering to have you constantly tell me you want to make love to me, and yet you've never—" She took a deep breath. "You've never asked me to marry you."

He was silent for a second. Then he took her hand once more and they walked along, going the other way, back toward the hotel. "If you want to know the truth," he said, "I've thought about it."

"Well?"

"I have feelings about crutches," he said. "I don't like them. I don't think a marriage always works out in the best interest of both parties."

"Oh," she said, and somewhere inside her the complicated feelings were beginning to circle themselves into just one emotion: shame. *How*, she wondered, *is a girl supposed to feel when she has just been told he won't marry her? He can say it in any way he wants; he still doesn't want to marry me.* "It's odd you should use that word." They passed a glaring sign that advertised naked women waiting on tables. "Crutches."

"Look," he told her, "I don't want to argue about basic things like a guy's freedom to ski down a mountain." He looked around them. "Let's get out of this, get a cab. Come on."

In the taxi he pulled her close to him and kissed her.

"Thorne—I don't want—I'm not going to the hotel with you."

"Who said anything about that? I want you to meet some friends of mine. We can stay the night there."

Before she could answer him, the cabdriver turned around and stared.

"Are you Gundersen, the skier?"

"I'm afraid so."

"Hey," he said, "I saw you in the Alps, on TV. You were great." He stopped for a light. "You going out to the usual place?"

"Just to the cabins in the back."

Jamie sat up very straight. "I'd like this cab to turn around and take me to my hotel," she said rather stiffly.

"Do me a favor," Thorne said to the driver, "Explain to this lady about where we're taking her. I don't want her to jump out of the car or anything, just because she happens to have nasty thoughts."

The cabby, a young man with a nice grin, gave her a quick glance.

"He's talking about Mountain Haven. It's a place for kids. Mr. Gundersen is their number one big brother."

"Guest cabins are in the back," Thorne told her. "In the morning you'll meet all the kids.

"It sounds very nice, but I'm afraid I have to get back. David will send out the police—he'll think I've been murdered in the wicked city. He told me every crook in the country comes here."

"He's right, lady." The cabby glanced at them in the rearview mirror. "Is that your husband, David?"

"Her boss," Thorne said. Please, Jamie, I want very much for you to meet them. It's too late now—that's why I thought we could stay there. It's very nice."

"Yes," the cabby said. "It's very nice."

Jamie smiled. "I'd like to, but my boss—"

"They're very special kids," Thorne said.

"They sure are." The cabby flashed her a look in the mirror. "They're blind."

She felt his hand move against hers, reaching for it.

"I'd love to meet them," she said, and she thought, *Let David fire me if he wants to. Let him think I'm an idiot to want to spend my time with a man bent on dying and a lot of blind kids!*

But of course the truth was David understood. It was only that he was afraid for her.

She settled back against the seat, close to Thorne's beating heart, as the cab drove out of town, toward the dark, silent desert.

CHAPTER XI

It was a strange but oddly happy day she spent the following day, with Thorne. She had slept well. Surprisingly, the guest cabins were roomy, warm, and the beds were just hard enough to ease the tension she'd had in her body. The couple who ran the place, Bud and Della, had appeared briefly in bathrobes, cheerful but obviously sleepy. They'd greeted Thorne warmly and said they'd see everybody in the morning, early.

Jamie was surprised, when she walked from her cabin to the wide patio in back of the low, one-story, red-tiled building, to find Thorne sitting out there, along with Bud, who wore a short-sleeved black shirt, black slacks and the turned-around collar of a minister.

Both men stood up. "Good morning," Thorne said warmly, "I didn't want to wake you. Coffee?"

She picked up a cup that looked handmade and held it out. The patio was an extremely pleasant place, with hanging plants, lush flowers, several birdbaths and low, comfortable chairs. Children were everywhere, tumbling in the chairs, hanging on the chair backs of Bud and Thorne, playing some kind of game with braille cards at a lawn table.

"My wife looked in on you," Bud said. "Lisa, don't pull at the lady's hair that way. Touch it if she doesn't mind, but don't pull."

"It's soft," the little girl said, and she turned her flower face up toward Jamie's. "Your hair is soft."

The child's eyes were pale gray and sightless. Suddenly, Jamie felt tears come to her own eyes. *What kind of man is this?* she thought, looking at Thorne. He was busy holding two small boys, one on each knee. Many of the children there were Indian, black-haired and brown-skinned and beautiful. They had been bought new shoes the day before, all of them, and it took quite awhile for all of them to come to Jamie to show off the shoes they could not see but were proud of nonetheless.

There was lunch at noon in the dining room, a cheerful, blue and white room with pots of flowers everywhere.

"The kids like to touch them," Della explained. She was thin, not pretty but glowing. It was easy to see that she was a girl who was totally satisfied with her man and her life-style.

"Have you been here long, at your school?"

Della smiled. "It isn't our school—Bud gets very upset when people say that. It's God's school. He was the one who brought us here." She handed another sandwich to the little girl on her lap, a child who wore glasses so thick that her eyes looked grotesque. "He laid a burden on us, as they say. Bud and I were happy as clams in the suburbs of Santa Barbara, California, when we suddenly weren't so happy. We'd taken a trip out here and visited a reservation where there were about ten blind children. It haunted Bud and me but we didn't want to admit it."

She poured milk for the child. "Now, here we are and here's the school, thanks to Thorne."

"Thorne!"

"Of course. He financed this place. Bud used to race boats and cars before he went into the ministry, and he'd met Thorne. He wrote a letter, got a phone call and—here we are, bless him."

But it wasn't just Thorne's money that had built the place; it was love. When she and Thorne left that afternoon, Jamie felt soothed, warmed, as if she'd been to some magic place, or had drunk some kind of magic wine.

"They loved you," he told her. "You were a smash hit."

They had taken a cab back to the edge of town, but from there, they had walked slowly, getting a ride in a pickup truck at one point, then walking again.

Now, they sat across from each other in a busy, brightly lit, all-night café. There were slot machines lined up against the wall and near the windows. People played them with a dedicated kind of intensity, as if they were spellbound by the machine.

It was a different world from what they had just left at the school.

"Do you suppose," she said, sipping her coffee, "Bud and Della would be happy doing anything else?"

"You mean like doing a song-and-dance act at one of the local clubs?"

"I mean anything else at all. She said God laid a burden on them."

"It's possible." He seemed somehow remote, as if a part of himself had left, departed. "Do me a favor, will you, when you get back to the hotel?"

"Aren't you coming?"

"I'm going back to Aspen. That makes more sense than staying here, now that I've seen the kids." He was, she realized, going, going, gone, leaving her as surely as if he had already got up from the table.

There was no use talking to him about Silverlode. He was determined to keep his date with destiny.

As she'd known he would be, David was up and all over the hotel, in the café, in the coffee shop, in the lobby, in the casino, looking for her. He looked as if he hadn't slept at all, when finally he spotted her in the lobby.

He hurried up to her, grabbing her arm.

"Are you okay," Jamie?"

"Of course I'm okay."

"You said you were going to be early. And you weren't in your room." He sounded accusing.

"I'm fine," she said, suddenly tired, weary, washed out. She had been so happy only such a short time before, with the blind children, with Thorne. Now that was all over. "I'd like to go to bed, if you don't need me."

"I'll see you at dinner, then." He stuck his head in the elevator door as she got on. "You were with him, weren't you?"

She nodded as the door closed. Why, she wondered, when she was once again in her hotel room, had she thought she could sleep? She wasn't sleepy, just worn out from worry, from the gigantic changes that had taken place in her life since that day David Saunders had hired her to go to work for him. She took a shower and then went to the window and looked out. Las Vegas never seemed to sleep; there seemed to be no clearly defined line between day and night. There were always people on the street; nothing seemed to shut down for the night or day.

It was a grown-up's world, an adult world, no place for children.

Suddenly she turned from the window. She hesitated for a moment, then she went to the phone and dialed the operator.

"Room twelve sixteen, please." She held her breath; Thorne might have gone straight to the airport to get a plane for Aspen.

"Yes?" It was, thank God, his voice.

"It's Jamie. I—I've been thinking about the children."

"What about them?" He sounded tired, as tired as she had felt a little while ago. No, she thought; it isn't fatigue. It's sadness. That's what I felt and that's what he's feeling now!

"I was thinking—I read somewhere that blind kids can be taught to ski, using Popsicle sticks. I know it sounds strange, but they let their fingers pretend they're legs, you see, to begin—"

"I've a plane to catch, Jamie. Take care."

She swallowed, tears behind her eyes. It was over.

"Yes," she said faintly. "Well—good-bye, Thorne. Good luck."

She went over to the bed and lay down on it. She didn't cry out loud, but tears came out of her eyes quietly, coursing down her cheeks. *God bless you and keep you safe, my darling!* David's birthday party began at eight, with Rhonda wearing a beautiful, low-cut white gown covered with sequins, showing off her figure to perfection. Jamie, in her simple green silk, felt out of place, but when a toast was made to David, she raised her wineglass and smiled at him. She was surprised when Rhonda came up to her, as the party was leaving the main dining room of the hotel, heading for a casino in another hotel down the Strip.

"Could I speak to you a moment?"

It was a surprising question; Rhonda had been very cool to her during the entire trip. Now she seemed anxious to be friends.

"Of course. Here?"

"No, in my room. I'm just down the hall from you."

They went up on the elevator together, not talking. Rhonda's room was like the others, large, impersonal, slightly gawdy in its furnishings. Her suitcase was on the bed; expensive clothes were everywhere, on chairs, even on the floor.

"I know what you must think of me," Rhonda said, lighting a cigarette. "You think I'm spoiled, selfish—"

It was the time to be completely honest.

"I think you're a woman in love with a man who happens to be too isolated in his grief to respond to you. I wish I could help you, but I know I can't."

The beautiful silvery eyes met hers. "Thank you. I talked to David last night, about you, about his feeling for you—about us." She looked, Jamie thought, not like a lovely, sophisticated woman who had everything in the world, but instead, in that moment, she looked very much like a small, lonely girl, trying to be understood. "I've known David for a long time. I knew his wife, and

I liked her. Everybody did. I guess—I thought that he'd get over her, but he hasn't. He never will. You see," she said softly, "I wanted to be the only love in his life." She was silent for a second. Then she looked directly at Jamie. "I've never been loved," she said, "not by anybody. Do you know what a terrible thing that is?"

The phone rang. It sounded like a scream, breaking the mood of sudden friendship that had come between them, somehow binding them.

"It's Freddie," Rhonda said, hanging up the phone. "He says everybody wants us to hurry up to the casino down at the Sands Hotel. They're all winning at blackjack." She picked up her small silver purse. "Time to go and have fun, Jamie."

"Yes," Jamie said, "time to go and have fun."

They waited silently for the elevator, both of them lost in their own lonely thoughts of the men they loved, men who did not seem to care about them enough to want to spend this evening with them.

Aspen was more crowded than ever, that next day, when Rhonda's private jet took them back there from Vegas. There was an air of anticipation about the place; people kept coming in on planes, in expensive sports cars, staying the weekend with friends or cousins, in order to be there when Thorne Gundersen made his daring try down Silverlode. Parties were being given; conversation at the coffee shop centered mostly on whether or not he would make it.

Emma had tea waiting for them when they got back. David's study had been cleaned; his book was finished and somehow the place looked very different.

"Ready to go to work, Jamie?" He settled himself at his desk, taking off his coat. "Now that I'm a year older, it's time to begin my next book. You can order paper, whatever you need, and we'll start right away." He looked at her in the dim light. "Unless, of course, you'd rather sit around and feel miserable. I've always found that work is a very good antidote—"

"David, what about your lecture? You said you thought that might stop him."

He leaned back in the chair, there at his desk. "It's scheduled for tomorrow night, and the press will be there. I told you I'd try, Jamie, and I will." He took out some notes from his pocket. "Now—I thought we'd begin with—"

"You think it's useless, then?"

"I don't think I or anybody else can stop a man from killing himself if he has his mind set to do it. Or if he's so hung up on proving what a hero he is that he'd die doing it."

She went to the window and looked out. A new snow was beginning to fall; the houses and streets looked clean and new. It was beautiful here, and in spite of what she'd seen at those parties and in Las Vegas, she'd never forget Aspen, with the Rocky Mountains framing it, presided over by the great Ajax.

"I'm quitting my job, David," she said quietly.

"You can't quit. I'm just starting another book and I need you." He came over to her. "I really do need you in my life, Jamie."

"You only think you do." She went over to her desk and began sorting out her things. "The truth is, David, you need a wife. I've told you that before. You need a *wife,* David."

His face was ashen, as if he couldn't believe she would quit, leave his house forever.

"I have a—"

Their eyes met. "Had," Jamie said gently. "Margo's dead, David, and you're just going to have to accept that. It doesn't mean you have to stop loving her, or that she'd want you to be lonely for the rest of your time here. David—Rhonda loves you, and she desperately needs you."

He had gone quite pale. He took off his glasses, wiped them on the corner of his old coat sweater, then put them back on. There were, surprisingly, tears glistening in his eyes.

"I've no desire to marry again," he said rather shortly. "None at all."

"You asked me to marry you. Weren't you serious?"

"Of course I was serious. But that was different."

"You mean because you happen to be in love with Rhonda, so you can't marry her. But since you aren't in love with me, that makes it perfectly all right to marry me. That way, you wouldn't be unfaithful to Margo."

"I'm asking you," he said stolidly, "not to leave. How can you expect me to carry on and go on with my work if you decide to go back to Minnesota?"

"Wisconsin."

"You're crazy," he said, and he shoved his hands into his pockets and began pacing the room. "Why couldn't you let things go on the way they were in the beginning? Why couldn't you be a nice little girl and type for me and not—not go falling in love with an idiot whose about to break his fool neck and not stand there telling me I ought to get married to Rhonda simply because I happen to love her very much!"

There was a silence as he realized what he had just said.

Their eyes met. "Go on," Jamie said softly, "go to her, David. Don't waste another single minute of your life without her."

"She's spoiled and she gives too many stupid parties and most of her friends are boring and nasty—" He let his breath out. "Okay. I know, I know. She's a little girl, really." He smiled. "I've always known that she's only a lonesome little girl."

"Aren't you going to do something about making her happy?"

He was lighting the gas jet at the fireplace. When he stood up, Jamie saw that his brown eyes were anxious.

"If you leave here and go home, Jamie, what's going to become of you?"

"I'll probably marry a very nice dairy farmer and have a lot of well-brought-up children. I'll be fine, thank you."

"So you're running out on him," David said.

She closed a desk drawer, neatly putting things on top.

"I'm not staying to see him die." She looked at David. "You know it isn't going to help, your lecture. And the petition—you found out they wouldn't sign it, didn't you, David? You just didn't want to tell me." He was looking very uncomfortable, she noticed. "You can't stop him, can you?"

"Jamie—there isn't time! I didn't want to tell you because I didn't want you to have to know just yet. I'm giving my lecture and press conference, announcing the emergency proposed ban on skiing that particular run, due to its reputation. But it isn't going to change anything, Jamie. He's still going to try it. I'm sorry," he said heavily. "Maybe if I hadn't been sitting around feeling sorry for myself, I'd have done something about it long ago—gotten people involved in putting a damned fence around that run and a No Trespassing sign on it."

"Did your doctor friend Mel say anything about Thorne that might—"

"It was a dinner party, Jamie, not an examining office. Tell you what—you go on up to bed and in the morning we'll discuss your quitting."

"No," she said firmly. "I meant it, David. I won't be here when Thorne goes down that mountain—I can't. I want to thank you for a lovely job." She went over and gently kissed his cheek. "Good-bye, David."

"Well I'll be damned," he said softly, "she means it."

She did indeed. There was no problem in finding another place to stay for the night; the bakery had been sold to a couple who were friends of Jamie's aunt and uncle. All it took was a visit to the baker, and over hot spice cake and coffee, she was invited to spend the night in her old room.

The nightmares she'd once had in this room, right after her Cousin Kurt was killed, came back to her this night. She had dreamed of watching a beautiful bird die in flight, falling to the ground, but tonight her dream was much more real than that.

She saw Thorne in her dream, poised, in the classic position for takeoff at the top of the ski run. He put one hand to his forehead suddenly, the way she had seen him do many times.

For some reason, this gesture struck terror into her heart.

She woke up bewildered, forgetting where she was, thinking she was in her cozy room at David's house. Then, realizing what had happened, she groped for her robe from her suitcase on the floor.

The room was chilly; she had forgotten that about it. She was trembling as she went to the window to shut it all the way. Then, suddenly, she found herself facing Ajax, in all its powerful beauty, standing there like some kind of reminder.

She closed her eyes. It was almost—as if the mountain were speaking to her, whispering to her—

His eyes! In the dream, he had rubbed his forehead; he'd done that often, increasingly often. And the broken glass and the bruise on his hand—those things surely meant he had bumped into things, had walked into the patio door, had bumped into furniture—

Oh, God, she thought, *oh, my God—Thorne is going blind! The man who loves blind children so much is going blind himself!*

And he wanted a try at Silverlode before that happened.

CHAPTER XII

It took quite a long time to rouse David; when he half stumbled down the stairs in his bathrobe, barefooted, he was scowling. He turned on the porch light and peered out. Then he yanked the door open, his face still angry.

"I'm glad you came to your senses, Jamie. Now come on in before you freeze us both." He led her into the hallway. "I'd have come to get you, you know. You didn't have to——"

"I didn't come back for my job or to stay with you, David." She was cold, cold and trembling. "I came back to ask you something, something you didn't tell me before." He was trying to get her damp coat off her, but she resisted. "David—when your friend Mel sat across from Thorne at that dinner party in Vegas, he saw something, didn't he?"

"I told you, dearest one, a doctor doesn't make a diagnosis on the basis of sitting across from someone at a party! Is that what you came back here to ask me? Because if it is, I'm going to toss you right back into the snow!"

"David," she said almost desperately, "you've got to tell me what Mel found—he looked at him, didn't he? I mean, he looked——"

"Of course he looked at him; I told you, they sat across the table from each other. Come on; I'll give you a brandy. It's quarter-past two in the morning, did you know that?"

They had reached his study, and as he began switching on lamps, causing the familiar room to fall into a soft glow, she put her hand on his arm, forcing him to pay attention to her.

"Mel looked into Thorne's eyes and they were red, weren't they? I used to think it was only that he'd been on the slopes and had gotten too much glare, or that he'd had something to drink at someone's party the night before. But that wasn't it, was it?"

"You'd better have a brandy," he said quietly, going to pour. "Here—and sit down. You were very foolish, you know, to come over here and get all upset this way, simply because your friends has red eyes. I have red eyes too, most of the time."

"David," she said evenly, "if you won't tell me the truth, I swear I'll call up Mel and ask him myself!"

"He's a doctor; he isn't going to give you any medical information."

"Then there *is* medical information!" The knowledge that she'd been right came upon her with renewed horror. "He's going blind," she said. Sudden tears clogged her voice. "And he can't face that, because like most of your people, David, he's really all alone. Nobody really cares much if he lives—he's just something beautiful for them to worship for a little while."

He eased her into a chair. "Mel cornered him after the meal and told him he wanted to talk to him. When Thorne didn't come back to the hotel—I guess you were with him—Mel waited until he did. Then he banged on his door and asked him a few questions. It had nothing to do with prying; he was concerned, as a doctor, about whether or not Thorne had seen anybody about his eyes. Mel still wasn't certain, of course, but he figured some tests would be in order."

"Thorne's going to take the tests?" That's crazy, she thought. He'll never make it down the mountain and he's thinking of getting his eyes checked—no; Thorne knows what it is that he has. He knows what's wrong with his vision— "He's taken tests already, hasn't he, David?" She let her breath out.

"Yes, weeks ago. It's uveitis, and he may or may not

be having a lot of pain. Sometimes it may be a passing thing and other times it might be very bad. According to Mel, there's usually blurred vision, but it's a thing where there will be recurrences." He reached for her trembling hands, taking the untouched glass from her. "They have drugs, medicines now that can very often control it. Only your friend apparently doesn't or can't accept the fact that it's happening. Frankly, I think he's scared, scared to death—of going blind."

"David," she said, hang on, trying to think of A Way. "David—we've got to stop him!"

"That's the point, Jamie. That's why I didn't tell you. We can't stop him. I'm going to announce at my press conference that a certain young man can't see and he's still going down Silverlode. That's overstepping my territory."

She stared at him unbelievingly. "Do you mean to say that you know Thorne can't see well enough to try that or any other run and you're not going to stop him? All you'd have to do is tell the newspaper people that, when you talk about your book and it's theme, and they'd see that he doesn't go down. David—you're helping to kill him!"

His eyes were steady, dark, somehow gentle. "What you don't seem to be able to understand, my dear child, is that each of us must be allowed some degree of absolute privacy, some private place to go with our souls and make decisions. Apparently, your friend has made his—he'd rather die than be blind. It's as simple as that. And I've no intention in the world of trying to force him to live if he chooses not to." He poured himself more brandy. "When does your flight leave, Jamie? I'll be glad to run you to the airport."

She felt dizzy, the way she'd felt when they told her Kurt was dead. The world, David's words, seemed far away; she was shut up in some tight, terrible world of horror. David, solid, good, yes, even loving, David, was telling her that it was the right thing to do, doing nothing. Watching Thorne die was not going to be very nice, so would she please hurry and go away on an airplane, back to Wisconsin, so she wouldn't have to watch?

"You're wrong," she said suddenly. She'd been sitting where he put her, sitting like a sad little child, when the thought came into her mind: *David is wrong. This time he is dead wrong!*

"I'm not wrong about his stubborn death wish, if that's what you mean."

"But you're wrong about—about letting him do it, not trying to stop him! David, when you say every person has a right to choose his or her time to die, you're wrong! Listen—we *owe* each other something! If Thorne or any other one of us decides to cop out, then there's no telling how many of us left behind will suffer because of that one, insane, totally selfish decision on his part. Do you realize what he'd be throwing away?"

David's eyes had gone dark; he looked at her with a totally new, mature kind of respect.

"You really believe that, don't you?"

"I *know* it! We all need each other, need love and kindness and understanding from each other. To murder love, or to simply ignore it when it's there, offered, waiting for you—that's not only sinful, it's foolish. I love Thorne; I want to spend my life making him happy. If he dies, he'll never give my love a chance to grow and become bigger and bigger and bigger. And there happen to be a lot of blind children that are going to lose a friend!" She had begun to cry; she had not wanted to cry in front of David, and here she was, doing just that. It wasn't the kind of crying she'd been likely to do before in her life, the kind that immobilizes; instead, it seemed to spark her with a fierce anger, some kind of desperate frustration. "You've got to stop it when you talk to the newspeople," she said again. "If you don't do that, you'll never be able to write another book that has anything at all valid to say, David. I mean that."

His face had gone a bit pale. Finally, he went over and poured himself another drink, a rather large one.

He was drinking again; he would never begin his new book if he did that. She suddenly saw him as a man who was losing, not gaining in life, not gathering love and prosperity to himself, but instead, a man who, for all his glib language and powerful prose, failed to see the real truth about life.

"I'll take you to the airport," he said finally, his voice remote. "If you're still planning to go back to Wisconsin, that is."

Jamie picked up her coat. "I'm not going back," she said quietly. "At least not now. Not until he's dead. I'll have a whole lifetime to go back there and grieve for him." Her voice was steady. "Good-bye, David."

He didn't answer her.

David's lecture and remarks about his forthcoming book, which had been purchased by a movie producer and was soon to be made into a film, shot in Aspen on location, took place as scheduled.

There was a tea afterward, according to the evening paper; Mr. Saunders had been in fine form, talking about the latest news that he'd been asked to do the screenplay on the upcoming film version of his book.

Not a word about Thorne, not a word about the petition he'd promised to circulate.

She was busy that evening, helping in the bakery, getting up early morning to help make the bread and rolls, the way she'd once done when her aunt and uncle owned the place. The Eikerts were a nice, serene couple who perhaps guessed that their unexpected young guest was going through a very private kind of agony.

On the night before the exhibition, Jamie sat up all night, curled in the wide window seat of the little attic room. There was a high, pure silver moon and the mountains shimmered in their snow blankets. The whole world, it seemed, looked especially beautiful, as if dressed for some very special happening.

Toward dawn, when already cars were lining up, people were finding places behind the guard ropes along the slopes, Jamie slept, her dark head buried in her arms.

The pounding on the door was so loud that she nearly fell off the window seat. There were voices, one of them unmistakably that of David.

Footsteps on the stairs then, and poor, little Mrs. Eikert was standing there looking bewildered and upset.

"Your former boss is downstairs with a lady and they want you right away. Emergency, he says. He might be drunk, but I don't think so. Shall I call the police?"

Jamie hadn't undressed; now she groped for her shoes, slid them on over her wool socks and hurried out into the upstairs hallway. She leaned over the railing and saw David, standing on first one foot and then the other, and Rhonda, who was wearing, weirdly enough, no coat and a fuzzy blue bathrobe.

"David—what on earth—"

"Get down here at once, dammit! Rhonda can tell you on the way."

Jamie ran down the stairs. They were hustling her, bundling her, kidnapping her, and taking her out the door of the bakery, past early-bird, startled customers, and on outside to David's car.

"Get in," Rhonda said, and gave Jamie a push. David jumped in the driver's seat, started the engine and roared off with such force that whatever Rhonda had been about to say was lost in the noise.

They were heading for the mountains, or, to be more specific, toward Ajax. Rhonda turned around and began talking, her voice quite loud, because something was wrong with the heater and it was making a loud noise.

"He's up at the Lodge. A reporter saw him and phoned David." And before Jamie could protest, say she didn't want to see Thorne, not now, not this one last time because the very fact that it was the last time angered her, Rhonda held up her hand.

A thin, old-fashioned wedding band was on her fin-

ger, the married finger, as her aunt would have said.
Rhonda, married!

"It happened yesterday," Rhonda said, smiling.
"David came over and told me he kept thinking about
something you'd said, about how it was a sin to throw
away love. And the next thing I knew, we flew to Vegas
and got married in one of those awful, commercial
chapels." She gave David a quick kiss on the ear.
"We're going to be married again, properly. In the same
church where my grandmother was married—for the
first time."

"I'm very happy for you both, I really am," Jamie
said. "But I'm not going up there to talk to Thorne, and
neither of you has any right at all to try to force me
to—"

"You see," Rhonda told her, as if Jamie hadn't spoken at all, "there was never anybody in my family who
understood that, who valued being loved. All my people
threw away husbands and wives and kids as if replacing
people with new people was perfectly sane. So of course
they were all miserable."

"What my beautiful wife is trying to get through to
you," David said, "is that we believe what you said.
Murdering love, ignoring it, that's just what Thorne is
doing if he goes down that mountain. But," he said,
"there's a reason. In this case, Thorne thinks he
wouldn't be acceptable any longer. He sees a dark room
where nobody wants him. The same thing is wrong with
him that was wrong with Rhonda—the poor guy doesn't
know the first thing about love, because if he did, he'd
kick this whole crazy thing down the tube." He looked
at Jamie, then back at the winding road. "The least you
can do," he said, "is tell him."

She got out of the car at the Lodge and walked up
the steps, not hurrying. People were lined on the wide
porch, standing with binoculars pressed against their
faces.

They obviously didn't know Thorne was at the
Lodge, so Jamie went straight to the bartender, a bored-

looking young man who spoke with a Southern accent.

"I'm looking for Mr. Gundersen, please."

"Go on outside, miss. That's what all them people are doin' out there, looking for him." He began putting peanuts into silver dishes. "It'll be on TV a little later on, though, so you can watch him and keep warm." He grinned. "It's a color set, so you'll be able to see the blood real good and all."

"He's here," she said, suddenly feeling desperate, "he's here in the Lodge, in one of the rooms. Someone saw him—please—"

"You a friend of his?"

"Yes, yes, I'm a friend of his."

"He's down in the private dining room section, by himself. Looked to me like he could use a woman; I don't think he's comin' back and I think he knows it."

She ignored the insult and hurried down the wide hallway, to the darker, smaller part of the building. She knocked on several doors, then began opening them. In one, a couple quickly jumped apart; in another, a maid glared at her suspiciously.

She found Thorne sitting in a deep chair in front of the fireplace in a room that had three small, intimate table settings for private parties.

She came up behind him, not touching him. "I know you don't want to see me," she said quietly, and he turned around, startled, then jumped to his feet. He was dressed, ready to go down the run, wearing his sky-blue ski clothes, the goggles hanging loosely around his neck.

"I hadn't planned on a last-ditch meeting," he said. "If you came here for a last shot at telling me to quit, be it known the answer remains the same. I think you'd better go, Jamie."

She took a small breath. "I love you," she said clearly, raising her chin. "I'm not In Love with you, or maybe I'm that, too, but most importantly, I love you, Thorne. Not because of anything but because I do. Because God has given us to each other and neither of us has a right to deny the other of that love. Do you understand that? Do you understand—that I'm telling you I want to be with you, whether or not you can see, or walk, or even talk. I love you. Please—don't hide from that!"

He looked stunned. The blue eyes darkened, and suddenly Jamie found herself staring at his broad back.

"Good-bye," he said. "Find yourself a nice dairy farmer."

She didn't remember walking out of there, out of the room, the Lodge, down the steps to where David and Rhonda waited in the car.

"Well?" David held the car door open for her.

"Can't you see she didn't get anywhere with him, idiot?" Rhonda put her arms around Jamie, there in the car. "Take us home, David—Jamie needs another woman with her for a while."

"No," Jamie said suddenly, and she sat up straighter. "I'm going up on the runs, to find a place to watch."

It was crowded, but because it had begun to snow again lightly, a damp snow, some people left choice spots to go to the Lodge and watch on television. Jamie stood a long time waiting, waiting for Thorne to appear.

When he did, it was suddenly; the lift had stopped sometime before, letting him out at Deadman's Peak, a run that was used for practice by the experts.

She was surprisingly near him; he glanced downward, and as if she were compelled, she raised her hand in a silent salute to him. The crowd, who had set up a mightly roar at the first glimpse of their blood hero, suddenly stopped making any sound at all. Thorne stood poised like a bird, ready to spring forward and then down, down Silverlode.

What happened then had a dreamlike sequence to it. Thorne suddenly straightened up, looked to one side and then stepped out of position and backward. Some sound went through the waiting crowd, a kind of murmur of disapproval, and then, as it became clear what he was doing—taking off his skis—they began yelling, shouting, cursing him. It was like a chant, the sound of them, calling to him to put on his skis again, to take off—

To die.

He moved toward her in the thick crowd, towering above most of them, pushing forward to get to her. When he did, with one had he took off his snow cap and with the other he pushed her body close to his own.

"I want to look at you every second," he said, his mouth against her wool cap; "I want to be able to remember how you look forever."

People were pushing toward them, asking questions, angry, some insulting. For a moment anger flashed in Thorne's face, but then, then, her hand went into his and together they began to walk toward the lift, not talking, past the crowd, to where Rhonda and David stood by their car.

"I think we should all get out of town for a few days," David said, shaking hands with Thorne.

Jamie climbed in beside Thorne, in the back.

"Are you ready to start talking some more about our kids?" She smiled at his look of surprise and pleasure. "I mean our blind kids. Thorne, I thought you could get right on their ski lessons, and maybe we could plan a tournament or something. And remember that house and vineyard you own, the one you never visit? Well, how about starting another school for blind kids there—"

His warm kiss silenced her, but only for a moment.

Dell's Delightful
Candlelight Romances

IN 1918 AMERICA FACED AN ENERGY CRISIS

An icy winter gripped the nation. Frozen harbors blocked the movement of coal. Businesses and factories closed. Homes went without heat Prices skyrocketed. It was America's first energy crisis now long since forgotten, like the winter of '76-'77 and the oil embargo of '73-'74. Unfortunately, forgetting a crisis doesn't solve the problems that cause it. Today, the country is relying too heavily on foreign oil. That reliance is costing us over $40 billion dollars a year Unless we conserve, the world will soon run out of oil, if we don't run out of money first. So the crises of the past may be forgotten, but the energy problems of today and tomorrow remain to be solved. The best solution is the simplest conservation. It's something every American can do.

ENERGY CONSERVATION -
IT'S YOUR CHANCE TO SAVE, AMERICA
Department of Energy, Washington, D.C